I0619675

Elevenses

a collection of sf/fantasy diversions

Don Sakers

ELEVENSES: a collection of sf/fantasy diversions
copyright © 2015, Speed-of-C Productions

All rights reserved

This is a work of fiction. All the characters and events
portrayed in this book are fictitious, and any resemblance to
real people or events is purely coincidental.

Published by
Speed-of-C Productions
811 Camp Meade Rd
Linthicum, MD 21090-3030

ISBN: 978-1-934754-18-4
June 2019

Dedicated to
Nancy, sister-in-law supreme
and Mike, nephew extraordinaire

Contents

Welcome

Science fiction and fantasy of different lengths offer different reading experiences. If a novel is a full-course meal, a sort story is more of a simple snack. A novel might take days or weeks to read, while one can often take in a short story in one sitting.

Some people are quick to dismiss both snacks and short stories as inconsequential; I'm not one of them. The midmorning snack, in particular, has a long and respectable history in many cultures around the world.

In the U.S. it's the venerable coffee break. In Sweden it's *fika*, in Australia *smoko* or *mornos*, and in the Netherlands *konkelstik*. In the Hispanic world it's known as *las onces*, and comes later in the day. Across the Commonwealth, morning tea is common. And in Britain and certain parts of Middle Earth, the term is elevenses.

No matter what you call it, elevenses is a time to pause and reflect, to visit and laugh, to have a bit to eat and a few morsels to fortify oneself for the challenges of the day.

That's how I hope you'll experience the eleven short pieces in this book: one each day, as a short break from your daily activities. Don't feel bound to read at precisely 11 am— elevenses is a state of mind, not a particular time of day. Also, there's no need to confine yourself to reading the stories in the order they appear here; skip around if you want, subject to your mood and the demands of your day.

With each story, I've included a suggestion for a food and drink combination that I feel matches the tale.

Of course, you're free to read any way you want. Devour the whole volume from beginning to end, read a story a week or one a month, read them backwards if you like. Ignore my culinary suggestions and substitute your own snacks. You're not going to hurt my feelings.

   With no further ado, here are my Elevenses. Enjoy!

-Don Sakers

The Real Thing

Menu: Rum-and-cola & honey-spiced almonds

Bar food seems appropriate for this story.

copyright © 2012, Don Sakers. Originally published in Unidentified Funny Objects, UFO Publishing, 2012.

"By rights, your species should be all but extinct and your planet totally uninhabitable."

The Ran'chit, three meters tall and the general shape and color of a giant cockroach, loomed over Jane with its clicking mandibles a hand-span from her face. Its breath reeked of week-old garbage and rum. It had been at the bar when she arrived, chain-swilling rum-and-colas—the preferred drink of bugs everywhere. Then something set it off, and it approached her. The other patrons, aliens all, turned politely away. With a sigh, Jane wondered what she'd done to deserve this.

Sixteen lightyears with a bum portside stardrive and a misbehaving waste disposal had left Jane with a headache only scotch could cure. With docking complete and cargobots unloading her ship, she holed up in the spacer's bar. She intended to sit in a corner and wait for her head to match the station's spin, while hoping something would turn up for tonight. Something male and reasonably intelligent, if possible. Instead, half an hour into her program, a more-than-slightly-blotto insect with an attitude the size of Saturn's rings was breathing rum-flavored rot into her face.

"Humans." The Ran'chit's translator managed a disgusted tone, a perfect counterpoint to clacking mandibles. "We should never have given you the stardrive. You should have been left to extinction on your own miserable Earth."

The bartender glanced at Jane, its metal face impassive. She shook her head slightly. This time of day, she was the only

Human in the place; all around the bar, others drew back in obvious anticipation of a spectacular fight.

Going up against a Ran'chit's six razor mandibles, armored hide and legendary speed was fairly low on Jane's list of priorities. She stood, facing the Ran'chit squarely. "Friend," she said, "I have no quarrel with you, and I hope you have none with me. I drink to your health." She raised her drink while the alien listened to its translator. But before she could take a sip, lightning-fast claws closed over her wrist.

"You stole our empire," the Ran'chit snarled.

Jane swallowed. No simple way out of this one. Those claws could easily sever her wrist, and the creature's face with its compound eyes and multiple mouths was already too close for comfort.

She yielded to the pressure, letting her captive arm go limp while at the same time moving her free hand toward her pocket. "I repeat, we have no quarrel. Kindly withdraw your appendage, and we will share ritual drink together."

"The only drink I desire, Human, is your blood."

That was it. A clear threat, witnessed not only by a dozen aliens but by the bar's servbots. The Compact was satisfied; Jane could act freely.

She pulled her free hand from her pocket and swung a small spray-bottle up to the Ran'chit's face. Before it could react, she squirted a few dozen milliliters right onto its antennae.

The creature released her, drew back, and huddled in upon itself. "I am sorry. I beg your forgiveness."

Warily, Jane returned the bottle to her pocket. Ran'chit Queen-juice was powerful stuff; the poor bugs had no choice but to obey, even worship, the one who wielded it. Best thing Earth ever came up with. For the next few hours at least, this Ran'chit was hers.

"You are forgiven. Return to your place."

It whimpered, a shriveled hulk of a bug cowering from her voice as it slinked back to the bar. For an instant, Jane felt sorry for it.

"We *did* take your empire, after all," she said. "But look what you were doing with it. Running around trolling for mature industrial races you could give the stardrive. So when their planets became uninhabitable, you'd have another few thousand slaves."

The Ran'chit cocked its head and looked for all the world like a sad-eyed beagle. "It was our destiny. So we had done for ages. So we did with your folk." The translator sounded wistful. "Humans did not follow the rules. Your Earth should have fallen victim to greenhouse effect. So went every other world we know."

Jane crossed her arms. "Yeah, well, it *didn't* happen to us. We beat the greenhouse effect." And with millions of Human traders to contend with, rather than a few thousand, your empire just couldn't take the strain. Poor bugs, you never had a chance.

And once synthetic Queen-juice came along, well, you literally had no choice but to sign the Compact. And open the rest of the galaxy to Earth's trade. Now the slave races are free and we all live happily ever after.

Except the bugs, drunks and dreamers, fewer of them every year.

The Ran'chit stared morosely into a half-empty glass. "How did you do it? No industrial civilization escapes the greenhouse effect. You burn fuel, pouring carbon dioxide into your atmosphere; you clear land, destroying plants that remove the carbon dioxide; within two centuries your planet's carbon balance is demolished and runaway warming takes your world."

The bug waved at the viewport, and the white-shrouded planet beyond. "Dead planets, all of them. Except for Earth. Earth survived. Earth *still* burns carbon-based fuels. How do you do it?" The bug sounded desperate, the living embodiment of every bug in the galaxy asking the same question. How?

Jane sipped her scotch. "It's a simple question of carbon dioxide." It wouldn't hurt to tell the poor bug; between rum and Queen-juice it wouldn't remember anything tomorrow. "The other greenhouse gases don't matter, there are too few of them. You've got to get rid of the excess CO_2."

All eyes, ears, and antennae in the place were on Jane now. She felt like an ancient priestess declaring the words of the gods. *If any of you had known this,* she thought, *your planets might be alive today.*

"By the end of the twentieth century we knew the trouble. All we had to do was figure a way to get excess carbon dioxide off Earth. Then you came along with the stardrive, and we had our answer.

"Earthers have always known what to do with our excess. If you can't eat it, burn it, or sleep on it...then you sell it." She shrugged. "That's all there was to it. We shipped our carbon dioxide off into your empire, more every year. And we followed in person. By the time you started to wonder what was going on, we were already in charge."

"Sold it?" The Ran'chit looked as if it were trying very hard to blink. "You *sold* your carbon dioxide?" It finished its drink with one gulp and a shudder.

"That's right," Jane nodded. "It was only a matter of finding the right product. It helped that we picked something that was habit-forming for Ran'chit as well as Humans." She signaled the bartender. It glided over on gleaming treads. "Let me buy you another. We'll drink together, and then I have to go." To another bar, another station, another world. Because, brother bug, I don't want to be around when you wake up from *this* bender.

The Ran'chit held out its glass, still lost in thought. "Sold us your carbon dioxide?"

Jane nodded at the bartender. "Another scotch, straight up. And a rum-and-cola for my friend here."

The bartender inserted a nozzle into the proffered glass, and a succession of liquids flowed. First rum, then heavy brown syrup, then finally tonic...spectacularly, gloriously effervescent tonic, foaming and bubbling, overflowing the glass.

AUTHOR'S NOTE

I got the idea behind this story at a party where the topic of global warming was on everyone's lips. For the record, I wasn't drinking rum-and-cola at the time; I believe it was a screwdriver. I may have to blame this one on my friend and fellow sf writer Melissa Scott—gin and tonic was her preferred tipple at the time.

When I heard that Alex Shvartsman was looking for humorous stories for the first of his highly-successful *Unidentified Funny Objects* anthologies, I sent him "The Real Thing" and got notice of acceptance immediately after.

My original version contained an additional line at the end to hammer home the point. Alex wisely convinced me that it was unnecessary. That's what good editors do.

Coco

Menu: Cocoa and strawberries with cream

Cocoa, of course. And strawberries & cream need no justification.

copyright © 1983, Don Sakers. Originally published in Fantasy Book, December 1983.

Her skin was so grey and desiccated that it looked like leather. She resembled an ancient voodoo doll, or one of those age-old mummies the museums were so fond of displaying. Her little remaining hair was white and fine, more like spidersilk than hair—almost as though cobwebs had gathered about the head. Wrinkled skin was stretched tight over very obvious bones. The lips were colorless, dry as the rest of her face. Her body was hidden by the covers of the bed on which she lay.

She looks dead, Llodes thought to himself. But why not? She was as old as some of those museum mummies. Only the terrible spells cast with the talismans and dusty bottles which filled the suite kept her alive at all.

Coco opened her eyes. They, too, were grey. Once, those eyes had been blue, but as time had passed, first years, then decades, then centuries, their color had faded like the ink on ancient parchments. Everything had faded. Only the brain was still strong, the lump of wrinkled grey tissue behind the wrinkled grey face. The eyes twitched once, then settled on Llodes. Cracked lips parted; then voice was nasal and scratchy. "What do you want?"

Llodes nodded his head in lieu of a formal bow. "The Oora have risen to mate. Our worlds are in danger. Itelt has fallen. Hala Gydig is under attack at this moment. You must do something."

She lay so still that Llodes feared she'd fallen asleep. Should he try to wake her? His stomach twisted in revulsion at the thought of touching that leathery skin. He was ready to call for an attendant when she spoke. "My mind wanders. Who are you?"

"I am Llodes hough Daascis, Khedive of the Council. You must help us."

"What is it you want me to do, Khedive Llodes?" The rasping voice was calm, undisturbed by the knowledge that humanity's ancient enemies were once again on the wing.

"The Oora are swarming. You must use the Casque. The Kaafi must be told to fly against the Oora. Time is short."

Llodes looked into the crystal bound at his wrist, and sighed at the war reports scribed there. Hala Gydig had all but fallen, and the Oora had been sighed on Espitloris. In his imagination Llodes saw the huge, falconlike Oora descending from the airless cold of space to feast on the warm bodies that awaited them in human cities. He could hear the screams as Oora beaks gutted their prey. He could also hear the anguished questions of panic-stricken mobs wondering why the Kaafi did not take wing to protect them. But without Coco's mind and the magic of the Casque prodding them the Kaafi would not leave their roosts.

She spoke. "Why should I help?"

Llodes was taken aback by the question. "You are Coco. You have always helped. For centuries—"

"For millennia," she corrected.

"For millennia, then, you have protected your people from the Oora. Why should you stop now?"

Again she paused. Llodes wanted to reach beneath the covers to grab her frail shoulders and shake them. Anything to make her see her duty.

"They are not my people," she said. "You know as well as I that I am not quite human. Your wizards have proven that. What care I for your people?"

He glanced again at his wrist. Swarms of Oora were moving into the heavily-populated areas of human space, moving through magical gateways and jumping from world to world. He saw a vanguard of brave fighters torn to pieces by the claws and beaks of the hostile creatures, wondering where their Kaafi saviors were.

"You were human once."

The voice quaked. "Perhaps. Perhaps long ago before I was locked up in this sub-basement, before the Casque was placed on my head and before it made me its own. That was thousands of years ago. That well-meaning child is gone now. Where has she gone?" Coco shook her head and seemed to drift. "For thousands of years I have directed the Kaafi to fly against the Oora. I have felt the cold of space and the blood-lust and the pains of death. I have lived for years and years between Oora mating times, waiting half-alive in the grip of your suspension spells for the time I could save you again. For hundreds of lifetimes I have lain here while Khedives and Councils and Worlds have come and gone." The old woman sighed. "I am tired. I wish to rest. If I am of no more use to you, perhaps you will cancel your spells and let me find rest at last, let me lay down the burden of all your lives. If not, then the Oora will free me when they come. I am old; I will feel little pain from their claws."

Llodes shook. She was serious! "There must be another way to control the Kaafi. If we could not find it? We could release you then, for we would have no more need of the Casque and its power."

"You have not tried, though. And as long as I am alive, as long as I exist to protect you, you will not try." The eyes closed. "I have told you, I have told Khedives before you for lifetimes, humans controlled the Kaafi before I came along. You must learn their language, you must treat them as equals, not as slaves to be dominated whenever Oora-mating comes."

"It will take years." Llodes found that he was almost pleading. Disgusting, that a man should be lowered to pleading with such a creature as this.

"You should have started years ago." Was that movement of the lips smile or grimace? It was hard to tell.

Llodes took a deep breath. He had no authority to act without orders from the Council. But if no one acted....

"Protect us this one last time, and I will order the wizards to dissolve their life-support spells. You may have your rest. And may you burn forever in Hell."

"I have already burned, Khedive. Hell would be a relief. What proof have I that you will keep your word?"

He spread his arms helplessly. "What can I offer you?"

"I will offer you a condition. Remember that I control the Kaafi. If you do not allow me to die once the Oora are gone, then I shall lead the Kaafi in full blood-lust against your worlds. And remember that the Kaafi are far stronger than the Oora."

Llodes shivered. "It shall be done."

Coco opened her eyes and stared straight ahead rather than at Llodes. Slowly, jerkily, the old head nodded. "I will help." The silvery Casque settled on the wispy hair, magical radiance dancing along its surface. Coco closed her eyes, and Llodes felt relief.

On a hundred worlds, the Kaafi stretched their wings and rose into the skies to do battle with their cousins, the Oora. There could be no doubt of the battle's outcome. It was a furious fight, and many of both races died, but in the end the Oora retreated to whatever cold wastes they called home. The Kaafi settled to their roosts once more, and on a hundred worlds humans breathed a collective sigh of thanksgiving.

In a deep, sheltered sub-basement on humankind's oldest world, a woman died...and a new age began.

AUTHOR'S NOTE

I wrote an early version of this story as an exercise in a college Creative Writing class. In this exercise, intended to spark creativity, students were each given a couple of words drawn randomly from a hat. Our assignment was to come up with an idea based on those words, then write the story. My two words were "Coco" and "eagles."

In that early version, the story was strictly science fiction, with Coco controlling the Kaafi via a mind-control helmet and kept alive for millennia by sophisticated medical technology.

I liked the tale enough that I polished it up and put it in my regular cycle of submissions to professional markets. In due time, all the SF markets had rejected it. There were a few fantasy-only markets on my list; I decided to turn the story into a fantasy. After all, the story contained some pretty advanced technology—and as Arthur C. Clarke tells us, "Any sufficiently advanced technology is indistinguishable from magic." (I have my own corollary to this statement, which states that any sufficiently primitive magic is indistinguishable from technology, but no one ever listens to me.)

Turning "Coco" into a magic-based fantasy story did the trick: it sold to *Fantasy Book* and was published in the December, 1983 issue of that magazine.

Purgatory

Menu: Chamomile tea and biscuits

Settle in and stay a while....

copyright © 1991, Don Sakers. Originally published in Analog, September 1991

I don't *think* I'm in Hell. The last time I checked, Satan's teleport code was unlisted. But you can never be sure about these things. Science is always making improvements in things, and for all I know International TelePortal signed a contract with the Vatican last week.

So maybe this *is* Hell. Or more likely it's Purgatory, where Auntie Dora was always sure I would wind up anyhow.

What else would you call it? It isn't exactly the dark, featureless limbo she promised. Dark is what you see when you close your eyes, and as near as I can tell I don't even *have* eyes. Or anything else, for that matter. Oh, well, she got the "featureless" part right.

There's *me*, at least. I can think. It takes an effort, like forcing yourself to stay awake in a warm room in the wee hours of your second all-nighter in a row. Much easier to say goodbye to thought and just drift. A lot like watching threevee.

Sorry about that. I faded for a while. Where was I? Right, I don't *think* I'm in Hell. The last time I checked, Satan's teleport code was unlisted....

No, no, no! That's how this place is, even when you force yourself to think, you keep coming back to the same place. Now I know how a cassette feels.

Back to the same place. And how did I get here?

Simple. I punched a code, then stepped through the public TelePortal at First Avenue and Thirty-Fifth Street. I was one step behind my partner, Cufflink Lenny. He's called Cufflink because that's the sort of loot he likes to acquire—every middleclass mark has a drawer of cufflinks, tie-tacks and tacky jeweled money-clips that he looks at once or twice a year. Any fence will give you good cash money for that stuff, and by the time the mark misses it, it's far too late.

Cufflink taught me almost everything I know about the business—retrieving teleport codes of solid upper-middleclass marks, where to find the best loot, wiping out your traces, dealing with the cops. All I added was my hacker's skill at breaking security codes.

Look at it from the mark's standpoint. You're rich enough to have your own TelePortal, instead of having to stand in line at the public station. Naturally you want the Portal in your house where you can show it off—but you don't want to give people like Cufflink and me access to your house.

So you put in a security feature. Give keys and codes to your closest friends. Anybody who doesn't have the key and know the code gets bounced to the public Portal nearest your house. Fundamentalists, bill collectors and petty thieves are out of luck.

Cufflink and I aren't petty.

We made out okay. We chose our marks with care, and I wrote a worm that watched each account and notified us when the whole family had 'ported out for the weekend. We live well, Cufflink and me, middleclass at least but without any hassle since we always deal in cash. Three successful jobs a week, and the rest of the time we live in luxury.

Or we *did*, until now.

I stepped through the TelePortal, and the next thing I remember is…nothingness.

Damn it, TelePortals aren't supposed to go wonky.

And what had happened to Cufflink? Did he do the job, or was he in his own little piece of Purgatory?

I'm right here with you, Bobby boy.

Cufflink?

I'm here.

I don't hear Cufflink—how can you hear without ears? His words are simply *here*, the way the words of a neon sign hang in front of you. Perhaps they've been here all along, and I haven't noticed until now.

Cuff, where the hell *are* we?

Don't you know?

I have my suspicions. *I don't suppose you ever met my Auntie Dora?*

What?

Never mind. The TelePortal malfunctioned, that's clear. And now we're stranded alone in—

Alone?

That voice isn't Cufflink's. I don't know how I can tell; you might as well say that it *sounds* different, although there's no such thing as sound in Purgatory. Call it taste, call it smell— whatever it is, I know that Cufflink and I aren't the only ones here.

Who's that?

Mary the Mouse, Bobby. Don't you remember me?

Sure I remember her. Mary the Mouse is one of our chief competitors. Half a dozen times in the last year we've gone on a job only to find the mark completely cleaned out. Nothing you could prove in court—of course not—but each time the grapevine said Mary had beaten us to the punch. We'd talked with her, off and on over the years, about combining our talents. Mary was never interested. The Mouse, she says, is a solitary animal.

Fancy meeting you here, Mary, I think toward her.

Uppermiddle mark family on vacation for two months? comes her answer. *Do you think the Mouse would let an opportunity like that slip away?*

So you were after the same marks we were?

I can almost feel her shake her head. *Poor Bobby. You still don't understand, do you?*

I feel like a schoolkid when everyone else gets the joke.

Cufflink says, *You don't suppose they'll be back early, do you?*

Mary gives a mouselike squeal of a snort. *Not bloody likely, friend. These marks have been saving for two years for this trip.*

What if they never come back? What if they're in a crash, or they like it so much they decide to stay?

Then we're in deep trouble, Cuffy.

Who? What?

Cufflink ignores me. *Do you think any others will show up?*

We're here...do you suppose Tank and the Butcher won't be along soon? And Lady Godiva?

If I had a head, I would shake it. *What are you two talking about? Tank and the Butcher are from Jersey, Lady Godiva's in Texas...they won't use the same defective Portal we did.*

There is almost a sense of compassion in Cufflink's answer. *Bobby Boy, we'd better talk.*

But there isn't time, because suddenly a change comes over the world. Everything has been motionless, unchanging—now that's over, and for an instant all Purgatory seems to be shifting, sliding, moving off in a strange direction and carrying us with it...

Mary the Mouse nods. *That'll be Tank coming in. The Butcher will be a few seconds behind him.*

What do you mean—? I start to ask, then the nonexistent air is filled with the bitter stench of teleportation, and a great voice fills our world. The voice of the uppermiddle homeowner who left his house empty for two months. Empty but not untended.

Damn it, International TelePortal could at least have *warned* us before introducing a new service....

The deafening, inescapable voice chants on:

"YOU HAVE REACHED THE KADOWSKI FAMILY. WE'RE NOT IN NOW, BUT AT THE SOUND OF THE BEEP YOUR TELEPORT PATTERN WILL BE RECORDED AND STORED UNTIL WE RETURN...."

AUTHOR'S NOTE

This is a gimmick story, riffing on an sf trope at least as old as Bester's *The Stars My Destination*. As with most gimmick stories, it's best not to think about this one too long or too deeply—if you do, improbabilities start to pile up , and soon the whole thing collapses under its own weight.

Still, it is a fun read.

Buying Time

Menu: Coffee and donuts

Just business.

copyright © 1999, Don Sakers. Originally published in Lower Than the Angels *(Lite Circle Books, 1999)*

"Graves must be stopped. The man is completely out of control!" Wilson slammed his fist down on the wrought-iron table, making all our drinks jump. I quickly rescued my gin-and-tonic before he could do it again. "He's purchased over two months just in the last week." Wilson's eyes flashed with that particular intensity which meant that very soon someone, somewhere would be sorry.

Cohen sipped his bourbon with a trembling hand. "He bought out Mahoney on Friday. Three hundred million." He lowered his voice. "Any one of us could be next. Any one."

I leaned back in my chair and stretched. It was a beautiful afternoon: the sun was bright and warm, but a few skittering clouds and a hint of chill in the breeze gave promise of an early autumn. All around us, the Berkshires hovered like mounds of bright candies: lemon, orange, raspberry and cherry. I sighed. It was altogether too nice a day to spend worrying about Graves and his machinations.

Takamatu steepled his fingers and stared straight ahead, striking the pose of a Zen master in deep concentration. His act fooled no one; Takamatu was third-generation New York. "Mr. Graves has betrayed the fundamental principles of our club. He has abused the trust that we placed in him. Action is necessary."

For long moments there was silence; then Smythe shook her head. "We seem to be agreed, gentlemen." She riffled a stack of printouts that documented Graves' abuses. "Only one question remains: What action can we possibly take? How can we touch him?"

Even Wilson had no answer for that one.

We had formed our little club three years earlier, when Dr. Ebert call us together to consider his unusual proposition. We were an even dozen then: twelve of the nation's leading business figures. None of us was in the top ten or even the top twenty-five; but all of us were hard-driving, success-oriented executives with that little extra spark that so many of our compatriots were missing. Call it devotion, call it innovation, call it the ability to stretch yourself beyond the proverbial extra mile—call it what you will, it was a quality that we all shared.

Ebert began quickly and deliberately. "Madam and gentlemen—how would you like to have some extra time in your lives? Time to spend with your loved ones, time to take in a show or a leisurely dinner...time to use in whatever way you see fit?"

Wilson had snorted. "Is this what you called us here for? A pitch for some time-management seminar?" He started to rise. "I have secretaries to deal with this sort of foolishness. Talk to them."

Ebert—short, fat Ebert with his bald head and his myopic squint—raised one hand. "Five minutes, sir. Five minutes is all I ask. Leave at the end of that time, if you must...but please, hear me out."

"Get on with it, then." Wilson glanced at his watch as if noting the exact second.

Ebert cleared his throat. "Consider, if you will, how much time goes to waste in this nation. 'Killing time,' it's called. A crime worse than murder. How often have you seen it: middle-class husbands collapsed in front of the television for hours each night? Old men and youngsters roaming the shopping malls, unable to devise any useful pursuit for their empty hours? Senior centers filled to the brim with decrepit crones who live on game shows and soap operas?" He spread his arms. "How often have you wished that all those excess hours could be put to good use? Have you ever wondered why you couldn't just purchase some time from those wasteful wretches, time to keep for yourself?"

Wilson glared.

Ebert gave a nod. "Now it can be done." He held out his wrist—it was adorned with a large, gaudy, yet somehow tasteful gold wristwatch. "I have developed this device to harness what I call the Ebert Effect." He smiled. "A little conceit on my part. What does it mean? Nothing short of a revolution, madam and gentlemen, a revolution in the way we treat time."

"Now look here —" Wilson began.

"A revolution," Ebert repeated. "With the Ebert Effect one can literally buy time, transfer it from one individual to another. There are plenty of people willing to sell a few free hours, if the price is right. One suburban shopping mall alone can supply a year's worth of time in a single summer afternoon."

"If you expect us to believe for a single instant that you can —"

Ebert's smile never wavered. "Mr. Wilson, would you be so kind as to consult your wristwatch? I wish to know how many of my five minutes remain."

Wilson looked down, then sputtered. I looked at my own watch.

Stopped.

"I've taken the liberty of buying a few hours for each of you. Call it a free sample."

"But…" Cohen looked out the window. The wind still blew, traffic still crawled down on Fifth Avenue, there was still the distant sound of phones and clatter from the offices outside this boardroom. "Time hasn't stopped…"

"Of course not. You are on…er…*borrowed* time at the moment. Go for a stroll. Take time to enjoy the sights and sounds of the city. When you return, everything will be as it is now, waiting for you."

Mahoney shook his head. "That's insane. Suppose I meet myself, going from one place to another? Won't there be some kind of explosion, or..."

Ebert only laughed. "Quite impossible, I assure you. The fabric of spacetime is remarkably resistant to paradox." He waved his fingers. "Go. Assure yourselves that this is no hoax. Smell the roses in the park. Return to your offices and enjoy some thinking time. I will be here when you return."

We split up, and it was just as Ebert had predicted: the world still continued to function, clocks and traffic continued to run, time continued its inexorable creep. And one by one, quite naturally, each of us found himself drawn back to the boardroom where Ebert waited, smiling.

Graves was the last one to return, a thoughtful look in his eye. As soon as he was seated, Ebert nodded and touched his wrist-device. "Two hours and eight minutes. I hope you all enjoyed your little vacation." He sat down at the head of the table and leaned forward on his elbows. "Gentlemen and madam, I'm prepared to sell you as much time as you may need, at only one hundred thousand dollars an hour. Now, are there any takers?"

We founded the club that very day, as soon as Ebert had fitted us with wrist-devices. It wouldn't do, Cohen pointed out, for us to use the time we bought for *work*—after all, we didn't want anyone getting curious about our little monopoly. What was the point to buying time if everyone could do the same?

So we agreed: we would not go overboard. We would use our bought time only for leisure activities: fishing, sailing, spending time with our families. Arbuthnot owned a resort in the mountains, and it became our most frequent hideaway.

Oh, I can't say that none of us used our extra hours for profit, once in a while. Temptation was difficult to resist: the vital meeting, the essential deadline about to be missed, the extra hour that meant the difference between success and failure in a fifty-million-dollar deal. Each of us had occasional lapses, of course. Along with our wrist-devices, Ebert gave us a central unit that printed records of everyone's time usage. So although each of us backslid, none abused the power any more than the others.

Until Graves.

"We have to cut him off. Shut down his device."

"Don't be stupid, Cohen. How are we going to do that? Throw him down on the ground and pull the thing off? Or do you want to call the cops?"

Cohen wilted. "We ought to talk to Ebert. Get *him* to do something."

"I have spoken with Dr. Ebert," said Takamatu. "He sees no reason to stop Graves. He does not feel that Graves is a threat." Again the steepled fingers. "I am afraid that the good Doctor has been seduced by money. He even mentioned," Takamatu paused for a moment, "that he is considering raising the price of hours to a million dollars each."

Cohen threw up his hands. "Graves can afford it. Why not, when he can make twenty million with each bought hour? But the rest of us—that's too rich for my blood."

I thought of my wife and grandchildren, waiting inside for Gramps to finish his business lunch. Of how dear they'd become to me in the past three years.

Wilson was right. Something had to be done.

"We'll buy *him* out, that's what we'll do," Smythe said, showing perfect teeth like unblemished ivory. "If we each do the same thing he's done, we can raise three, four, five billion in the next month. And give Graves a taste of his own medicine."

"No," said Cohen. "Then it would be you next, Elizabeth. Or Wilson, or Arbuthnot. And we'd never be able to stop." He shook his head. "No. I'd rather go broke, than get on *that* treadmill."

"You may have your way, Ira," she countered.

I picked up the printouts. "Two months last week. Fifty days the week before. Sixty-two the week before that." I'd be damned if I'd let Graves steal my family from me. "He's been doing this since last December. And it's taken us until August to realize what's going on."

"Well we've realized now. What are we going to do?"

I drained my gin-and-tonic and sat back in my chair with a grin. "I have an idea. But I need to make a few phone calls first." I glanced at my wrist-device and did some quick mental figuring. "Will you spot me...oh, half an hour each should do it?"

Takamatu, Wilson and Smythe agreed at once; Cohen gulped, then nodded. "You're sure this will work?"

"No surety this side of the grave," I answered. "Except one." The joke was lost on them. "Never mind. Just contact the other members, and have them all meet here tomorrow. On the prick of noon." I rose.

"Graves, too?" Wilson's eyes met mine.

"No. I'll take care of Graves." I put on my hat. "Until tomorrow." Then, before they could ask any more questions, I left.

I was glad to see that they were all early.

Only six members of the club remained—six plus myself and Graves. They sat around an outdoor table in their various states of agitation, ranging from Arbuthnot's near-comatose to Cohen's positively fidgety. I was the seventh in the party, my guest the eighth. I gestured for him to sit down, but pointedly did not introduce him.

The last echoes of a distant village church bell were dying when Graves appeared. As always, his dark suit was impeccable, his jeweled ring tasteful, his black hair in a perfect cut. No one witnessed his arrival; he was just suddenly *there*, leaning on a table and holding a scotch—no water—in one relaxed hand. "Well, my friends," he said, "I suppose I am wondering why you called me here today?"

"I suppose you already know," said Wilson.

"I suppose I do." He sipped his scotch. "The pity of it is that you can't do a single thing to stop me. Not without blowing the whistle on yourselves and revealing the Ebert Effect to the world."

"Perhaps not," I answered. "Perhaps we just want to give you a chance to recognize the error or your ways before it's too late." I waved at the printouts, which my guest had already examined in great detail. "Since January this year you've used three and a half years of purchased time. You've broken the agreement that we each made when we formed this club. You've used all that time for business—for profit. As poor Mahoney, Greer, Berke and Parker could testify." I have an open, honest face...but I did my best to narrow my eyes. "Just how much *have* you made in the last year?"

"Two and a half billion," he answered, without a trace of remorse. "And it's only August. I'll buy *all* of you out by year's end."

Wilson started to respond, but I silenced him with a glance. I looked back at Graves. "Thomas, aren't you even the slightest bit sorry? Don't you regret what you've done?"

"Not a bit."

"Has it been worth it for you—living four years in the course of one, working nonstop, three-hundred-hour weeks?"

He grinned. "More than you'll ever know." He looked from face to face. "This is survival of the fittest. And you, you poor sods, you're the dinosaurs. There's nothing you can do to stop me. It's," and here he laughed, "it's only a matter of time."

I sighed. He'd had his chance. Now I had to do what I'd planned, much as I hated to see it happen to anyone—even Graves.

"Thomas," I said, "I've been remiss in my hospitality. I haven't introduced you to my guest." All eyes turned to the one unfamiliar figure in our group, a severe young man in an ill-fitting suit and a clip-on tie. "This is Rafael Garcia. Or I should say, Special Agent Rafael Garcia." And then, for what Graves had done to Mahoney, I waited an endless moment before I finished: "Of the Internal Revenue Service."

Garcia flashed his ID. "Mr. Graves, I'm afraid that the Service would like to ask you to come in for questioning."

"On what grounds?"

"Tax evasion. It seems that you haven't filed a tax return for four years."

"That's ridiculous. I filed in April..." The truth hit him, and even Wilson had to turn away from the terror in Graves' eyes. "April. Oh my God. It's...been...four...years..."

Garcia had deputies standing by; they removed Graves' wrist-device before they carried him away. And I sat down heavily, accepting the drink I was handed without even wondering what it was.

Wilson laughed. "He was so sure he had us," he said. "So all-fired sure."

I grinned. "Nothing is sure, Wilson, except death. And, thank God, taxes."

Then seven of the nation's wealthiest business leaders, for the first time in history, raised a toast to the IRS.

It was a beautiful day.

AUTHOR'S NOTE

You've seen them at the mall: kids hanging around, goofing off, wasting time. And you've probably wondered what those kids could accomplish, if only their time could be turned to productive uses. I certainly did. And from that thought, it was only a short trip to "Buying Time."

When the folks at Lite Circle Books invited me to be part of their anthology of Maryland-area sf/fantasy writers, this story came in handy.

The Finagle Fiasco

Menu: Mulled cider and spice cake

Because what could possibly go wrong...?

copyright (c) 1983, Don Sakers. Originally published in Space Gamer, Nov/Dec 1983

Yes, I remember the Murphy episode. Of course, I was not Grand Master of Euler at the time—I was only Assistant Christensen Professor of Topology. Still, I don't suppose anyone will ever forget that time, when the Math Institute here on Euler was all that stood between the Galaxy and total domination by a sadistic megalomaniac.

What's that? Oh, yes, I know the Psychology Institute has done penance for allowing Khar-Davii to take over. And I understand that they say it can never happen again. Well, I wonder—psychology is not of course an exact discipline, like math.

Eh? Yes, the Murphy episode. As I recall, it was shortly after the spring term had begun. I had trouble with some of my displays: the Twenty-Dimension Simulator had developed a singularity, and simply would not accept fields with more than eighty operations. Maintenance told me that the entire system would have to be shut down for reprogramming, and I went to the Grand Master for approval. She was conversing on the hyperwave; I waited until she was done. In due time she opened the privacy hood and smiled at me. "Ah, Professor Yagwn. How are you?"

"Fine, Madam. And yourself?"

She sighed. "I could be better, Yagwn. You've heard of this Khar-Davii, who calls himself the Conqueror? Well, it appears that he has taken over the Galactic Council and killed the Coordinator. He has proclaimed himself Monarch of

Humanity, and the inhabited worlds are falling all over their own feet to surrender to him."

I recalled hearing something about the matter on the news. "Are his weapons that formidable?"

"Apparently so. Euler is the only planet that has not yielded. I was just talking with the outlying Galactic Traffic station—Khar-Davii's fleet is even now headed toward this world." She glanced at a data screen on her desk. "Ah, excuse me. The fleet has arrived. We are surrounded."

I had no opportunity to voice an opinion. There was a bright flash of light, and suddenly the image of a corpulent human man appeared in the center of the Grand Master's office. Behind him were banks of machinery tended by warriors in full battle dress.

"I am Khar-Davii, the Conqueror. Your miserable planet has refused to accept my rule. You will surrender to me now or I will destroy your world."

I suppressed a grin; the Grand Master did not bother to hide her amusement. "I hardly think it a miserable world. I rather like it. Conqueror, your plan of conquest would interfere with our spring term, and I'm sure that the commotion would upset many of our scholars."

Khar-Davii narrowed his brows. "As I was told—you are totally out of touch with the real universe. Mathematicians and philosophers—not a practical being in the bunch."

The Grand Master lost her smile. One thing that has always bothered her was the accusation that Euler is out of touch with reality. To her, math was the highest form of reality. She stood and faced Khar-Davii.

"My dear Conqueror, I will not allow you to bother Euler. If you wish to attack, then do so—but let me show you something of our defenses first." She touched a button, and a screen behind her showed the image of a great cannon.

I drew in my breath sharply at the sight.

"And what is that machine, Grand Master?" Khar-Davii asked with a smile. "Will it shoot strings of numbers at us?"

The Grand Master answered with another smile. "No doubt, Conqueror, a man with your military background has heard of Murphy's laws? That which can go wrong, *will* go wrong. Here we have them formulated as a theorem, and implemented as a weapon."

"And this is your defense?"

She spread her hands and regarded him as though he were a simpleton—which seemed readily apparent. "Long ago we investigated the Murphy Laws completely. This Machine amplifies their effects. If you attack us, your guns will fail to fire, your ships will suffer instrument breakdowns, your most trusted officers will trip and accidentally sound recall orders. You could never beat us."

Khar-Davii dissolved in a fit of laughter. "My fleet has been listening to this conversation—now they know what 'terrible weapon' Euler will use against them." He stopped chuckling. "Grand Master, prepare for your death. Fleet—Attack!"

The attack did not last long.

Since I had a little time to spare, I watched it on the viewscreens from the Grand Master's office. After twenty minutes or so, only the Conqueror's flagship was left in fighting condition. It was not too long afterward that Khar-Davii's image reappeared in the office. The Conqueror was harried and bedraggled, and there was fear in his eyes.

"Can I help you, Conqueror?" the Grand Master asked.

"Enough. Enough. Turn off that machine. We will sue for peace. I will not attack your planet any more."

"Fine." She pressed another button. "Your treaty has been logged. We have other weapons that we can use against you, should you try to break your word. I will thank you now to take the remnants of your fleet away without bothering us... we have important work to do."

"You will not try to prevent me from ruling the Galaxy? Your Murphy Machine is a more formidable weapon than any I possess."

She smiled. "Poor, poor Conqueror. You should have taken more mathematics classes. Deductive reasoning would have helped you. The Murphy Machine worked perfectly—as soon as it was turned on, things started to go wrong. The first problem that developed, of course, was the failure of the Machine itself."

"Failure...?"

"Yes." She laughed. "It was the superstition of your crews that defeated you, Khar-Davii. They believed that they could not win, and so they did not."

Khar-Davii snarled, and his image faded. Viewscreens showed his ships limping away from Euler.

"We shall have no more trouble from him. The memory of his defeat and his fear of a recurrence will prevent him from returning. He will attempt to rule the Galaxy and will forget about Euler." She shook her head. "What can I do for you, Yagwn?"

"I need permission to shut down the Twenty-Dimension Simulator for reprogramming."

"Very well. I will make the necessary notifications."

"Thank you." I turned to go, then paused at the door. "About the Murphy Machine. Do you think it was kind to lie to him so?"

"Kinder than letting him know what a terrible power he is really up against. He thinks the Machine unworkable." She shrugged. "Let *him* figure out why his empire dissolves so quickly."

Dismissing me, she bent her head back to her work.

AUTHOR'S NOTE

My Bachelor's Degree is in Math, and this is one of the most math-inspired stories I've ever done. First published in 1987, it was reprinted in the 1987 Arbor House anthology *Mathenauts*.

Originally, it was my intention to do a whole series of stories set on the math-centric world of Euler. One of these days, when I get the time....

Escape Velocity

Menu: Chai and brownies

Spice, caffeine, and sugar to get up to speed.

copyright © 1982, Don Sakers. Originally published in Analog, October 1982

"You're certain?"

"Gentlebeings of the press, there is no doubt. We've checked independently with both our large computers, Aristarchus and Kidenas. I'd better let them tell you."

"Charon Observatory has detected increased radiation from Sagittarius. The center of our galaxy exploded centuries ago. Radiation is now reaching us, and will soon make Earth uninhabitable."

"How soon?"

"Twelve hundred years. The last ships of the evacuation fleet should be launched within the millennium."

"Evacuation fleet?"

"Yes. We will move the Solar System's population to the Andromeda Galaxy. Our test probe leaves in three months."

It'll never work, Kidenas said.

It has to. The new gravitic drive can accelerate the ship to any fraction of lightspeed. They'll reach Andromeda after only a few years subjective. The ship presents minimum cross-section to interstellar medium—it's only twelve meters across at the widest.

And six hundred long; I know. The parameters are unassailable, Aristarchus. I still have a horrible feeling it won't work. We ought to explore other options.

Nevertheless, Probe One left on schedule. Aristarchus and Kidenas watched it velocity climb. After a few years it was 99%

lightspeed; then 99.9%, then the nines multiplied under the tireless gravitic drive.

Only the computers could think quickly enough to catch the probe's messages—and after a century, even they couldn't keep up with the time contraction.

We'll hear from them in a few hundred thousand years when they decelerate for final approach, Aristarchus said. *Let's get the fleet going.*

Kidenas had to agree…yet he couldn't shake his dread.

Eight hundred years later Probe Four Billion Eighteen left carrying the last humans, and Aristarchus and Kidenas sat back to contemplate an empty Solar System.

Probe One velocity is ten-exponent-minus-47 percent short of lightspeed, Aristarchus reported gleefully. Such minor variations had long since passed beyond the sensing capability of their most delicate instruments, but they could still be calculated.

Right, Kidenas answered. *And her mass is larger than Jupiter's, her length a minor fraction of a centimeter.*

Do you still doubt that the fleet was a good idea?

Doesn't matter. We can't contact the probes anyhow. And yet….

Kidenas threw some figures, didn't like the answer, and threw some more. *Oh God.*

What?

More massive than three Jupiters. Infinitesimally flat. And twelve meters in cross-sectional diameter.

Damn.

Aristarchus, they're within their own Schwarzchild radius!

Over the next thousand years, as Earth became steadily more uninhabitable, the two computers watched in horror as, one at a time, the ships of the evacuation fleet turned into black holes….

AUTHOR'S NOTE

Analog occasionally publishes what they call "Probability Zero" stories—very short stories that sound plausible yet are ultimately based on absurdities. I consciously wrote "Escape Velocity" as a Probability Zero story, and the editor agreed. It's a gimmick story, constructed around the intersection of relativistic physics and the dynamics of black holes, and if none of that means anything to you, then I doubt you'll find the story very engaging.

This was my first sale to *Analog*. The acceptance letter was typical *Analog*: after agreeing to buy the story, the editor continued: "I assume that you've computed the Schwarzschild radius of a three-Jupiter mass, and it's less than six meters?"

Well, *yeah*. Otherwise, it kinda kills the joke.

Cycles

Menu: Earl grey and banana nut muffins

Something hearty for the long term

copyright © 1985, Don Sakers. Originally published in Analog, January 1985

At first there was no space.

How could there be? The Cosmic Egg was crammed with the potential for mass-energy, but it was all undifferentiated. No manifestation so gross as *particles* had formed yet. With no way to distinguish parts of it from one another, there was no space.

No space, no time. Just formlessness seething with what would become energy.

Kaishyy had hardly admired his handiwork, when natural law asserted itself and the Cosmic Egg blew up.

Kaishyy's fellows paused in their own work for a moment, and one of them sneered derisively. "Well, you got it to explode. I'm surprised."

"What do you mean?" Kaishyy said as sweetly as he could manage.

"There's not enough mass-energy in it," the other said. "Oh, it might be pretty now, but soon enough it'll spread out and get uninteresting. It'll never collapse and become cyclic."

Another novice joined the taunting. "You mean Kaishyy's made an open universe? Too bad, Kaishyy—you'll make a fool of yourself in front of the Masters."

Kaishyy gave his own private grin, and turned toward contemplation of his infant cosmos without giving the others an answer.

Changes happened too quickly to make any impression, as the universe expanded and newly-formed time ticked off interval after interval. Particles formed—photons, neutrinos, quarks, and then whole classes of lesser particles. By the time the first second had passed, neutrinos dropped out of thermal equilibrium and neutrons were forming. The distinction between matter and energy was beginning to make its presence felt in a shadowy sense.

It took a few more minutes before the temperature had dropped far enough to allow atomic nuclei to form. Abruptly a threshold was passed and they began forming all over the place. In seconds all the free neutrons were snapped up, and the universe was a dense cloud of alpha particles, beta particles, and energy.

Kaishyy felt the presence of a Master behind him, and looked around. The Master gave a tolerant gesture. "Not enough mass-energy for collapse, Kaishyy. An open universe is of no use to anyone. Do you wish to start over?"

Kaishyy shook his head. "I will stay with this one."

The other nodded. "Your decision. But I feel it a waste of time."

"Thank you for your opinion, Master."

Kaishyy's universe had cooled appreciably by now, about five minutes after its creation. Kaishyy relaxed and looked further along the course of time—nothing much of interest would happen for a while.

Seven hundred thousand years after Creation, stable atoms began to form in Kaishyy's cosmos. In only a few centuries the brilliant blaze of light subsided and his universe became transparent. This result ran quickly through the experimentation area, and for a moment Kaishyy was the center of attention.

"Hey, Kaishyy, how'd you do that? Mine hasn't even begun to make atoms yet."

Kaishyy smiled. "Yours is too massive. Mine cooled much more quickly."

Hodal made a rude gesture. "Ours will collapse, though. You'll see. We'll get better remarks from the Masters."

"We shall see," Kaishyy said, and went back to watching his project.

Interesting things developed—stars, galaxies, quasars, all manner of complex forms of matter and energy Kaishyy watched for quite a while. The universe continued to expand, slowing slightly as it went but not at a rate that would lead to ultimate collapse.

After five or six billion years life developed in one of Kaishyy's galaxies. He looked around for his companions, to convey this news—but they were all busy with the atoms that had come about in their own universes, so he left them alone. Kaishyy simply watched, amused by the antics of his little creatures.

The little creatures provided Kaishyy with many diversions. In the meantime, some of his comrades' universes developed life of their own...but when he took the time to look, Kaishyy decided that *their* life was dull and sluggish compared to his.

After merely 10^{12} years, Hobal let out a great cheer and Kaishyy looked over to see what had happened. Hobal's universe, a very massive one, had begun to collapse and it blazed with energy.

Hobal looked rather apologetically at Kaishyy. "Sorry, friend."

Kaishyy waved. "Don't worry. Good luck with the Masters."

In no time at all, it seemed, Hobal's universe had collapsed back to its original spaceless, timeless potential mass-energy. A Master stood by and gave a nod at the appropriate instant. "If you do not shut it down, it will continue to oscillate, getting larger each time."

Hobal wiped out his Cosmic Egg and then, grinning like a fool, followed the Master away from the experimentation area.

Kaishyy sighed, and went back to his universe.

Life continued, which pleased him, but his universe was having troubles. One at a time, the pretty stars were winking out, or destroying themselves in tremendous explosions. And collapsars were forming in alarming numbers. Kaishyy knitted his brow and contemplated deeper. And there was a Master at his side.

"It is still not too late to start over, Kaishyy," the Master said graciously.

"No thank you. I stand by my project."

"As you will."

After 10^{14} years, all of Kaishyy's beautiful stars were gone. A number of other universes had collapsed in the interim, and their owners had gone with the Masters.

But now, at least, everyone was having problems with their stars. Before too long, Kaishyy thought with satisfaction, all the other universes will be dark.

Although the stars were dark, they continued to move... and in their motion, they kept sweeping close to one another. Each encounter did some damage—threw away planets, perhaps, or catapulted stars out of their galaxies. Or, even worse, made stars spiral down into the massive collapsars that had formed at the center of Kaishyy's galaxies.

He shook his head at the trend, but continued to watch. By the time 10^{18} years had passed, all his galaxies had evaporated and his universe consisted of dead stars, cold wandering planets, and black holes. Most matter was, by this time, iron.

Still life persisted, living on residual radiation and what it could extract from the still-energetic zones around collapsars. Kaishyy felt a little warmer when he observed living beings huddled around his collapsars—none of the other would have living things as long as he would. The collapse of a universe, of course, destroyed all life.

Kaishyy watched, as time ticked on and more and more of his fellows completed their projects. Finally, about 10^{30} years after he'd started, there were only a handful of the least massive universes left. And Kaishyy noticed a disturbing trend in his own cosmos.

For the first time he felt uneasy, and looked up for the guidance of a Master. At once one was with him. "What is it, Kaishyy?"

Kaishyy gestured to his universe. "The protons and neutrons are decaying."

"They *do* that, after long enough."

"Why wasn't I told?"

"Nobody ever thought you would make an *open* universe. Most closed universes don't stay around long enough for proton decay to set in."

"It's not fair."

"Kaishyy, you chose to work in applied cosmology—you have to accept natural laws the way they are." The Master shrugged and, not unkindly, said, "If you had started with more mass-energy...."

"Never mind. I still say my universe is interesting."

"But rapidly becoming less so." The Master left Kaishyy with his product.

After 10^{32} years all his protons and neutrons were gone, and his universe consisted of nothing but collapsars, photons, neutrinos, and a thin haze of electrons and positrons.

One by one, all of the other universes around him collapsed back to their Cosmic Eggs, and the students left. Finally, about 10^{50} years after the beginning, Kaishyy was alone in the experimentation area.

"Kaishyy," he heard, and turned to see Hobal in the form of a minor Master.

"So you're a Master now, eh? Good show, Hobal."

"Listen to me, Kaishyy. What you've made is useless. It'll never collapse; it'll just keep expanding until it's gone completely. Look how big it is *now*. Give up, start over, and in a fraction of the time you've wasted you can complete you project."

"All the Masters do it that way, Hobal. Well, I happen to think my way is also right. Look at this." He pointed.

"What?"

"There. Even with all the protons decayed, life continued. They've managed to draw their thoughts in photon and neutrino patterns, taking energy from collapsars."

"Life. The rest of us are Masters now. Do you know how embarrassing it is to have you still down here? And fooling around with life, yet."

"The Masters watch, Hobal. They will judge me. But not until my project is over."

"All of your friends are Masters now, Kaishyy. We're going to be among those watching you. And believe me, we can't let you get good remarks for a shoddy project like this."

"Oh, go away, Hobal."

Hobal left, and Kaishyy watched his cosmos expand.

Now and again, there was a bright flash, and these puzzled Kaishyy until he caught one in formation. Ah, yes, the collapsars were evaporating. He remembered something about that. Well, let them evaporate. Who needed them, anyway?

Alone, Kaishyy watched and watched. When 10^{100} years had passed, the last collapsar was gone, and he sighed. They had been exciting in their demise, at least.

Life, however, continued. It clung to patterns in photons that were becoming more and more red-shifted as the universe expanded.

After 10^{125} years, all the positron-electron pairs had collided and annihilated one another in showers of photons. Somewhere in the interim all the neutrinos had decayed—they were so hard to spot that Kaishyy had missed their departure. Now there were only photons, endlessly spreading in wavefronts that carried the last furtive thoughts of life.

Kaishyy was aware of attention upon him, the attention of the Masters. The question, he knew, was no longer "What will Kaishyy's universe do," but rather "How long will Kaishyy sit there?"

At 10^{200} years, Kaishyy's photons began to decay. Less energetic particles formed, their wavelengths blurring outward to fill his universe. Now even life was in danger, for no possible organization could hope to survive this sort of decay.

At 10^{250} years, long after the last coherent thought had winked out in his cosmos, Kaishyy put a stasis on his project and turned to face the assembled Masters. "My experiment nears its end," Kaishyy said. "I hope you will all attend."

"He's gone mad," Hobal said.

Kaishyy ignored the comment, pointed to his cosmos. "Look. All particles of energy have been decaying. Their wavelengths are now just about the size of my universe. Watch as I let the process continue for a few googol years."

Stasis released, time continued to flow. And the particles spread out, out—until their theoretical size filled the bloated boundaries of Kaishyy's universe. Now there were, in effect, no more particles—only the potential of mass-energy.

In Kaishyy's universe, 10^{250} years after creation, there was no space. How could there be? It was crammed with the potential of mass-energy, all undifferentiated. No manifestation so gross as *particles* remained.

No space, no time, just formlessness seething with what had been energy.

Kaishyy smiled. "Conditions are now identical with the beginning of my experiment."

Hardly had he made the statement, than natural law asserted itself, and Kaishyy's universe blew up.

In the distance, the oldest and wisest of the Masters radiated satisfaction. To this one Kaishyy bowed. "Master of Masters, if my experiment is run enough times, the life that it produces may manage to free itself from the bonds of its universe before photon decay sets in. Am I right, Master, in conjecturing that this is where *we* came from?"

The Master gave a benevolent nod.

Kaishyy grinned in self-satisfaction and looked over the others. "You see, an open universe *can* be interesting." Then he turned his back on them all, and attended to his creation.

Particles began to form....

AUTHOR'S NOTE

This is pretty much a pure "Analog story." This story grew out of two perverse impulses on my part. The first was my intuitive feeling that both sides of the greatest argument in modern cosmology—Closed Universe vs. Open Universe—were fundamentally talking about the same thing. The second was my desire to use the phrase "applied cosmology" in a story.

In my science fiction, I like to work with what's called "Deep Time"—I only feel comfortable when I have a minimum of ten or twenty thousand years to play with, and my Scattered Worlds series covers several billion years. But in "Cycles" I managed to go deeper into Deep Time than ever before or since. (I had particular fun throwing away the line, "…as I let the process continue for a few googol years.")

The Man Who Traveled in Rocketships

Menu: Milk and bread with honey

Comfort food.

copyright © 1990, Don Sakers. Originally published in Carmen Miranda's Ghost is Haunting Space Station Three, Baen 1990

The door dilated, and through it stepped a buxom, redheaded nurse. "Time for your medication, Mr. Riverside."

The man on the bed looked up from his terminal. Hairless, shriveled, face lined with age and taut with pain—yet his clear eyes were bright with the fires of intelligence and passion for life. It took a moment for those eyes to focus; it was as if he had been someplace far away, beyond beige hospital walls and the grey night outside. He gave a little sigh, then hit the "SAVE" key and pushed his terminal away.

The nurse gave her best professional smile. "What are you working on, another story?"

Riverside harumphed. "I wasn't aware that *we* were working on anything, my dear."

Her smile remained, but the slight drop of her eyes let Riverside know that his joke had gone too far. ""I'm sorry, Nurse. I'm an old man and very tired of being in bed. Please forgive me, and don't take my ill feelings for ill manners."

She brightened immediately. "Oh, don't mind me, sir. I shouldn't have—"

He forced a smile, tiny and fleeting as it was. "No, don't say any more." He gestured to her hypo. "What is Doctor Kelly giving me now? Horse tranquilizers?"

"Just something to help the pain." She moved in closer, and despite himself Riverside drew back. "Don't worry, it won't hurt. I'm good at this."

"Cooperate with the inevitable, I always say." He rolled over and she drew down the sheet.

As she rubbed the target with alcohol, she said, "I hope you don't mind my asking about your work. I've read all your books. That's why I requested this assignment. My boyfriend, he's your biggest fan. He even signed up to be an astronaut; he's wanted to go into space since he read *Have Rocketship, Will Travel*." The moment of injection was almost imperceptible. As she capped the hypo, Riverside turned and pulled the sheet up again.

"Well, thank you for the praise, my dear. And for being so understanding of an old man. This is a nothing, really—a short tale set on a place called Space Station Three." He reached for the terminal. "I hope you don't mind, but I want to finish this thought before I fall asleep."

"Of course." She walked to the door, then paused and looked back. A trick of light made her eyes twinkle. "I hope you'll let me read this one, when it's done."

"I promise you, you'll be the first."

She left then, and Riverside switched on the terminal. Bad as the pain was, it was almost preferable to sedatives. It wouldn't be long now before he fell asleep—but he had to finish this scene.

The middle of the night was the worst. The wee hours between midnight and dawn had always been his friend, and now their emptiness and silence turned them into an enemy. He stared into the darkness of his room, shivering a little with the waves of pain that came with every breath.

He willed his dreams, but this time they did not answer his call. Always before they had been there, swimming right behind his eyes, ready to take him away from the world and carry him out into space, to faraway planets and distant futures. Always before, he had been able to see the destiny of mankind, and it gave him more comfort than all the tranquilizers ever devised.

Now, the dreams would not come on command. And he was alone in the dark.

With a sigh, he reached for the television switch. Worse than mindless, an opiate...but perhaps it would put him to sleep.

It was an old movie, in gaudy color, with a forgotten film star of yesterday dancing across the screen under a turban that dripped fresh fruit. Now what was her name? Funny, how the memory was the first thing to go...Carmen Miranda, that was it.

Riverside leaned back against his pillows, seeking the least uncomfortable position, and tried to lose himself in the silly movie with its idiot plot. Soon enough, the remote control fell from relaxed fingers and his breathing became deep and slow.

Carmen Miranda danced across the sky, finally stepping into a familiar setting—the imagined corridors and pressure volumes of his own Space Station Three.

Asleep, he smiled. The dreams were back....

The nurse's name, astonishingly, was Jinny—"Like Jimmy," she said, "but with two n's instead"—and she was actually rather good company. Every once in a while, in the tilt of her head or a stray movement of her hand, he caught an echo of his *own* Ginny, gone these many years. The memories brought a lump to his throat...but he did his best not to let her know. It would only upset her for no reason.

"Oscar—that's my boyfriend—is training for space construction work. He's hoping to get a berth on the team for Space Station Two."

"I wish him all the luck in the world, dear. And what will *you* do, if he goes up yonder?"

She shrugged. "I don't know."

"Two is supposed to have residential space, you know. They'll need permanent settlers. Wherever mankind goes, there will be a need for nurses."

A slight blush touched her cheek. The TV, forgotten, rambled to itself in the corner. "Mr. Riverside, I'm not sure I could do that. I mean, to leave home and all...and the dangers...."

"Jinny, pioneers throughout the ages have faced the same choices. Tell me, were your grandparents born here?"

"No, sir. All four of them were immigrants. Two from Germany, one from Russia and my Grandma came from Mexico."

He nodded. "Then *they* made the same choice. You come from good stock, girl. Don't doubt your abilities." He raised a hand and gestured beyond the ceiling. "That's the future, up there. Not on this sorry globe. I only wish I was twenty years younger...I'd go in an instant."

She giggled. "You sound like Oscar."

"Listen to him, dear. Listen to me. We know—eh? Is that the President?"

She spun to the TV. "Yes, I think it is."

"Turn it up, would you? I'd like to know what he's doing to us now."

The familiar voice boomed forth, "...deficit projections growing, and in order to finance the Medicaid system, I have only one choice. My predecessor committed the wealth of this nation to pie-in-the-sky, but this nation can no longer afford such luxuries. Therefore, effective immediately, I am issuing an executive order to bring a halt to the civilian space program. Eliminating the costly development of Space Station Two will save us over two hundred billion dollars in the next decade— recalling the crews of Station One will raise that saving to nearly a quarter of a trillion dollars."

The President smiled. "All functions of the National Aeronautics and Space Administration will be transferred to the Department of Defense. I have instructed Secretary Miller to move forward as quickly as possible in replacing all manned missions with less expensive unmanned machinery.

"My fellow Americans, I hope you will join with me in welcoming the dawn of a new era, an era in which concern for our fellow citizens takes precedence over industrial greed, in which...."

Riverside waved, and Jinny, understanding, turned the set off. He settled back in his bed, and the expression on his face was one of sorrow, more intense than she'd ever seen on any human face.

"Mr. Riverside? Do you want me to—"

"If you don't mind, Jinny, I think I'd like to be alone now."

"I could get you—"

His eyes held sorrow, and the embarrassment of a man who wants to cry but needs privacy. "Please?"

"Of course. Just hit the button if you need me."

He said nothing more, and she retracted the door as gently as she could. Just before it clicked shut, she thought she heard a rattling sound. Maracas?

She shook her head. It was probably the sound of his keyboard—he typed so fast. She sighed, then walked to the floor station. "Alice? If Mr. Riverside gets any calls...let me talk to them first, okay? He wants them held."

It was the least she could do.

Kelly and Garcia were among the best doctors in the country; Jinny knew that Garcia had personally served two presidents and four governors, while Kelly was a double Nobel laureate. Still, she couldn't force confidence. Not even the best doctors could save a patient who didn't want to live any longer—and she had seen Riverside's hollow eyes and pale face before on other patients, just before they....

Garcia straightened and closed the oxygen tent over his patient. Tall and dark-haired, he was quite the handsomest doctor she'd served under for a long time. She couldn't resist stepping out of her professional persona for a moment. "Doctor, will he...what are the chances?"

"I shouldn't be telling you this, Nurse—but in his present condition I don't expect the patient to last the night."

She brushed away tears and was shocked to see them echoed on Garcia's cheeks. "Is…is there anything I can do?"

Kelly, old bald Doctor Kelly who could make a roomful of interns quiver with just a glance, put an arm around her shoulder. "The Shuttle fleet is permanently grounded, Space Station One is being abandoned, and the staff of Moonbase has been recalled. If the damned politicians would reverse those actions, I believe we could save him." He shook his head. "Otherwise…what does he have to live for?"

"It's not *fair!*"

"The universe isn't fair, Jinny my girl." Kelly glanced back at Riverside's indistinct form under its sheltering layers of plastic sheeting. "You know, if it wasn't for him, I wouldn't have gone into science. I'd have been a stockbroker, or an English teacher." He clenched his fists. "I've never felt so damned *helpless.*"

"Come on," Garcia said, "I told Maureen to set up a conference call with that Australian. Maybe we can learn something."

Kelly wiped his eyes and nodded. "Stay with him, Nurse."

The two doctors left, and Jinny sat down next to Riverside. She idly touched his terminal, then called up the story he'd been working on. He'd let her read a it, just yesterday—she sent the cursor to the end of the file and was disappointed to see that he hadn't added any more.

"Mr. Riverside," she said, "can't you hear me? It's Jinny. You've *got* to get better, sir. You have a story to finish. I want to know what happens on Space Station Three."

There was no answer…only the slow, labored breathing.

Riverside woke, and looked around the dark room. The hiss of oxygen, the intermittent beep from some piece of equipment and the pain. It hurt, even, to breathe. It hurt to think.

I'm dying, he thought. So this is what it feels like. I thought at least there would be release from the pain.

"Silly man, you are not dying."

Hands parted the oxygen tent, and there she was: Carmen Miranda, in a sparkling, sequined outfit which was like the eternal gleam of the stars from space. Her headdress held, not fruit, but silvery moons and ringed planets and a sleek spaceship poised for takeoff....

"Now I know I'm dying," he croaked. "I've never imagined you before. You're not one of my characters...."

"Meester Riverside, you do not imagine me. I am, how you would say, ze ghost. I am from se world of theengs that never were."

"Please...I'm so tired. I just want to rest."

"Ees not that easy, Meester Riverside. You have seen so much that I never see: Computers. Lasers. Apollo. But ees more to come. You die now, you weell miss so much."

He shook his head, slowly, each motion a study in agony. "No. Nothing left. Stupid children, they've given up their birthright."

"Silly, silly man." She retreated, to the sound of clicking maracas.

"Wait. Stay with me. I'm...afraid."

She turned her back on him. He raised himself up, felt IV tubes pulling loose from hsi arms, and didn't care. "Stay. Come back. Wait!" He reached for her, and in that moment she turned back. Pale hands touched his, and then there was the worst pain of all, like a pile driver going through his skull....

Riverside lurched, then fell back to the bed. And there was nothing but the pitiful squeal of a machine with nothing left to measure.

Jinny burst through the door and threw on the lights, but she already knew what she would find. The remotes told the whole story.

He was dead, all right...still warm, but beyond the reach of any emergency procedures. Somehow, despite years of training, she felt that it would be a sacrilege to try.

His face—his face, for the first time since the President's press conference, was untroubled...relaxed...and the impression of a smile played around the corners of his mouth.

Without knowing what she did, she reached for his terminal, punched in the appropriate codes. Then, hands shaking, she put it down on the bedside table.

There was no trace of the story he'd been working on. It was wiped, gone into the ether, and Space Station Three was no more, only a ghost of what might have been.

Ignoring her tears, she reached for the call button. "Maureen? Find Doctor Kelly. I don't care if you have to wake him up, get him into Mr. Riverside's room at once."

She put the button down, then rested her hand on Riverside's chest. "Thank you," she whispered.

Riverside gasped and Carmen Miranda slipped her arms around him. "Madam," he said, "I am not accustomed to such personal liberty from a woman as young as yourself."

"Shut up, you sill man, and let me leeft you."

"No, I'm too heavy—" But he wasn't; she lifted him off the bed without any effort at all. Behind her, he sensed...a presence. Something immensely old, terribly wise...and Old One?

The dreams were back.

"Ees no dream, Meester Riverside. Hold on, now."

He put his arms around her neck, amazed at how quickly the pain faded. He hadn't felt so good in years. *Decades!*

Then the hospital fell away, and he felt cool wind on his face, then dampness of clouds on his cheeks—and then Earth was below him, an intensely blue globe whose light made him ache. *We pray for one last landing*, he thought, but then the thought was interrupted as something approached from dark space: a great wheel, spinning in a stately gavotte among the searing stars.

I know this place. He reached for his terminal, then remembered that it was back on Earth.

The steel bulkhead seemed to part before them, and then Carmen Miranda lowered him, and his feet lightly touched deckplates. Around him, the floor and ceiling curved off into the distance, and the walls were broken by windows that showed black sky and bright stars.

Carmen Miranda stepped back and Riverside stood, unsteady in the lower gravity. "Madam, where *are* we?"

She giggled. "Another world of ghosts. The place of things that will never be."

"I know this place…."

"Yes, John. It's Space Station Three."

The voice was familiar, and he turned in surprise. There she was, tall and slender, her long red hair falling free and her green eyes a-sparkle.

"Ginny!" They were together in an instant, hugging so tightly that for a moment he couldn't breathe. The lips he thought he'd never kiss again settled on his, and their touch was like the finest wine….

"We've been waiting for you, John," she said, drawing back slightly. "We've all been waiting for you."

She waved around the room, and Riverside became aware that it was crowded with faces he recognized. Ellison, Christa, Judy, Dick…Gus…and others he knew well, John, and "Doc," and Leigh, and Cliff….

Then Ginny laughed, and took his hand, and the others closed around him in the warm embrace of friends.

Outside, the stars burned bright as Space Station Three spun on into the endless night.

AUTHOR'S NOTE

On Sunday, May 8, 1988, Robert A. Heinlein died. Without him, the face of science fiction would have been vastly different. Doubtless, when the first settlers arrive at Luna City on the Moon, or Marsport, or Alpha Centauri...Heinlein's books will be in their ebook libraries. His influence will live forever.

This is one of two stories I wrote for the anthology *Carmen Miranda's Ghost is Haunting Space Station Three*. (The other was "Tarawa Rising.") And yes, there was a time when $250 billion looked like a lot of money.

The Geas Ingenerate

Menu: Madeira and fine chocolate

Only the best.

copyright © 2013, Don Sakers. Originally published in Galactic Creatures, Sparkito Press, 2013.

They call me Will, but in truth my name is Erwilian; an ancient name that falls strangely on today's ear. It is a traditional family name, borne by many of my ancestors as far back as our records go.

For generations beyond count my folk have lived in this village of Montrose, one of the largest on this world we call Selenda. Because we tend the power springs and flows, we bear the age-old name Trician; go back as far as you will in the annals of Montrose, and you will find Tricians.

In most ways we are ordinary, traditional folk. Like every other family in the village, we have paid our tithes, fostered our share of foundlings, and taken our turns caring for Sleepers. Tricians have always served in the fire brigade and on the Village Council; my great-great granddam was Mayor. We dance at festivals and play on ball teams, we sing in choirs, and we always lend a hand when there's a barn to raise, a house to be painted, or a child missing in the forest. In most ways, we live our lives in the age-old patterns dictated by the Eternal Ones.

In one way, though, we are different. For among those in my family who share a bloodline—not counting fosterlings and adoptees but children of the body, as we say—among these there is an occasional one with what oldsters call the second sight, or the weirding way. Some say it comes from dealing so closely with the paths of power, others that it is a gift from the Fae. Some call it is a curse, and would shun those who display it.

My mother had the sight, as did two of her uncles. Sometimes it skips a generation, sometimes there are several in the family at once. It is something we seldom speak of to outsiders. But it is real, and I know for I have it too.

We speak of the Fae, the Eternal Ones, as if they lived long ages ago, in vanished places. Know, then, that this is not true: the Fae live now, and sometimes move among us. I have seen them, clearly as I see you here—heard their airy voices, looked into their fathomless eyes. And I was there on a night, many dozens of years ago, when one of them saved our world.

It began late on a midsummer night, when the ruby sun rode high in the southern sky, a sparkling mote bathing the night in cold carmine light that turned faces sanguine and leaves sable. I had spent the day up in the Wirren Hills, at the fire watchtower, which in those days was managed by three of the older Aedan teenagers, one born and two fostered. They were without power and it took me the better part of the afternoon to track down and repair a break in the conduits. With the power returned, the boys insisted that I celebrate with them, and I was mighty dry after all that work, so I stayed for a flagon or two and a few happy songs.

By the time I set off for home, the golden sun was long gone and the forest was deep with crimson shadows. Pearce's Mead, which just three days before had teemed with people at Midsummer's Faire, was a breeze-rippled sea of rusty turf. As I made my way past the lingering detritus of the Faire, remnants of booths and tatters of pennants, a shadow crossed the ruby sun. It being a cloudless night, I glanced up...and beheld a sight most amazing.

There in the sky, athwart the ruby sun and drifting slowly as the laziest cloud, was the shape of a springing cat, black as sunless midnight and with glowing viridescent eyes. Enthralled, I stopped and watched the cat slowly swing about, until its eyes seemed to light square upon me. Then without sound, without breath, without moving its mighty muscles, it came toward me.

I stood rooted to the ground, not in fear but in amazement. I felt no threat from the giant beast, neither malice nor menace, only a dispassionate presence, as if the creature looked right through me, interested only in the yard beyond me. It swelled until it loomed overhead, the size of the village square itself, blocking out sky and the forest, so close overhead that I could have reached up and stroked its sleek black belly.

Before me, the creature's belly split apart, spilling white light, and I shielded my eyes with my hand. Like a tongue, a slender ramp extended and touched the ground just meters from my feet. And a woman stepped down the ramp.

Revelation came upon me with the light, blinding and marvelous: this was no cat, no impossible creature from a giant's realm: this was a ship, a mighty starship fashioned in the guise of a monstrous feline.

The starships I knew, trade vessels which touched every few years on the rocky plains across the river, were clearly artifacts: constructed and assembled, contraptions of ceramic and metal with great exposed engines throbbing with suppressed power barely on the threshold of sensation, and crewed by rough, husky women and men whose language was coarse and uncouth. This craft was nothing of the sort; it was a wraith, still and silent as it crouched above the ground, not touching a single hillock but unmoving as the ancient hills themselves. Surely this gargantuan cat was not built, but conceived, not manufactured but grown, shaped by will and thought, given substance by art itself.

And the woman . . . .

Surely nothing less than a dark demigod, she was the very embodiment of night: mahogany her skin and chestnut her flowing hair, her raiment like shadow and smoke, now a shroud of sable, now a stygian cloak twinkling with a thousand stars. She was tall, nearly two meters, sylph-slender, and she moved like a regal panther, her bearing firm and unalterable. I knew at once that she was of the Fae.

I had seen them before, hither and yon, moving like phantoms on the outskirts of the village or passing with the express trains, and I knew that they were used to being invisible. My mother and my uncles had taught me to behave as if I, too, did not see them; neither to stare nor to avert my eyes, but to continue about my business. "Don't acknowledge them," mother said, "and they won't acknowledge you. This is the way."

Yet that night, beneath the great cat in Pearce's Mead and face-to-face with this woman of the Fae, I could not look away, could not pretend I did not see. She turned her head toward me and, as if a dark veil parted, I saw her eyes.

Sapphire and emerald they were, the deep slate of stormy sea, the dark evergreen of timeless forests, the aching azure of our world from space. Her eyes, as they met mine, were all of these—and much, much more. The flash of green at sunrise, the metallic cobalt of dragon beetles, the frozen blue of measureless arctic ice . . . those eyes caught me with a shock like no electrical discharge I'd ever felt, and I was enthralled, beguiled, mesmerized. In an instant, I knew that whatever this woman bade, I would do.

She lifted her eyes and spoke, her voice deep and resonant, yet hardly above a whisper. "*Greymalkin*, go. Wait in the hills. Come when I call."

Soundlessly, swiftly, the great cat sprang into the sky, and in seconds it was gone. The woman lowered her gaze once more to me, then without another word turned and walked toward the town.

I followed, moving a few steps behind her, as if I were in a dream.

By the time we reached the village I had come to my senses, and I strode as if she were not there, as if I were simply returning from an errand as I did so often. But always I walked in her wake, and even as I greeted neighbors and townsfolk, I kept part of my attention on her.

It was a warm evening, and it seemed half the town was abroad in the streets or milling about the square. The mysterious woman walked straight to the square, moving through the crowd and past adults and children alike without diverting her path, without taking any notice that they were there.

For their part, none of the others saw her or sensed her in any way. She might as well have been a phantom, or a hallucination to my eyes only. She towered over most of them, but they never noticed as she moved among them.

Business was good at the Tavern of the Moon; Maeve had all the outside tables set up, about half of them filled with raucous groups. The tall woman wove her way between tables and past patrons, right up to the bar; and there she stood, immobile, as one by one, four flagons rose and filled themselves with Maeve's best pale ale.

She turned and calmly strode out of the tavern, to the periphery of crowd, where two tables stood empty a few meters from the grand fountain that dominates the square. The four filled flagons followed her, floating unsupported in the air, while no one but me paid any mind whatsoever.

She stood at one table, then met my eyes and nodded at the other, only a meter away. My will and my muscles were not my own; I sat, facing her but also looking upon the dancing fountain beyond her. One of the flagons floated by, coming to rest on the scarred wooden table before me; the other three settled before her. Keeping her eyes upon me, she sat too, straight-backed and elegant. She glanced at my flagon, then back to my face. I lifted the heavy flagon and sipped at the cold, strong ale, all the time wondering if I were in a dream. She looked in one direction and another, then back at me. She lifted a single stately finger to her lips and narrowed her eyebrows slightly, then lowered her finger and looked away.

The town clock ponderously tolled eight, the deep knell of the big bell sounding in my ear like the woman's voice in the night. I glanced at the tower, as one does, and when I looked back two men stood before the woman.

Both of them, I saw at a glance, were Fae as well. One was short and bald, with a bit of a paunch and dressed in a severe sepia suit. The other was tall as the woman, with broad shoulders and close-cropped dark grey hair; he wore an unfamiliar outfit that nevertheless shouted its purpose: a military uniform of maroon turned almost purple by the wan light of the ruby sun.

No one took any notice of the newcomers, so I pretended not to see them as well. Instead, I kept my attention on the fountain, and sipped my ale as if I were waiting for a tardy friend.

The bald one gave a slight bow. "Telena Hoister!" he said. "I haven't seen you for an age." His voice was light, with a touch of an unfamiliar accent that flattened his vowels.

"Odilon Cooke," she said flatly, acknowledging his presence with a nod. She looked at the tall man. "You must be Admiral Dimi Luellen, hero of Ekladon. A fine bit of strategy there."

The tall one nodded. "I see that my reputation precedes me. As does yours, Maximus Hoister."

She smiled, gesturing to chairs. "Just 'Telena,' please. Sit down, fellows. Have either of you been to Montrose before? No? I think you'll enjoy the local ale; it's the best in kiloparsecs. If not for the horrible impropriety, I'd commission someone to bottle it and bring it to Terratwo."

The two men sat, tall Luellen with the same comfortable grace as Telena, and bald Cooke looking distinctly uncomfortable. "I'm not in the habit," he said, "of consorting with *Mundanes*." He looked about. "Are you sure they don't know we're here?"

The slightest frown crossed Telena's face for the barest instant. "Of course they don't. They *can't*. To them, we're empty air. If we touch them as we move among them, it's the wind. If we speak, it's a barking dog or a whistling bird. You could bed one of them, and they'd dismiss it as an incubus in a dream."

Cooke hunched over his untouched flagon. "It's eerie. I don't like tempting fate like this, Telena."

She chuckled, the sound of ice tinkling in crystal goblets. "That's because you've never served in the Loops. Believe me, the Geas Ingenerate is enforced by the eternal vigilance of a million telepaths channeling ten billion insensate familiars. It permeates space throughout this galaxy. You might as well worry about the reliability of nuclear forces or gravity."

Luellen, the tall one, stretched and swallowed a mouthful of ale. "Blast, that *is* good." He smiled. "When we control this planet, we're going to have to look into exporting some of it."

Telena leaned back slightly, catching both men in her gaze. "That's what I summoned you both here to discuss."

Luellen drank again. "Why *here*, of all places?"

She shrugged. "I want this conversation to be off the record. Can you think of a better place than a Mundane village on a disputed world? The rest of the galaxy pays no attention, and the Mundanes can't. It's just the three of us."

Cooke frowned. "Why us? What business do you have with us?"

She continued looking directly at them, until both men lowered their eyes. "Odilon, you're chief negotiator for the Federation in this region. Dimi, you have absolute command of Rebel forces in this theater." She put her elbows on the table and steepled her fingers. "I want both of you to leave Selenda alone. Carry out your war on other fronts, but let this planet be."

Cooke narrowed his eyes. "Selenda's not a Hoister Kindred world."

She cocked her head slightly. "No, it isn't. It's Convocation —which means no single Kindred has control."

Raising an eyebrow, he asked, "You come with orders from the Convocation, then? Why not send them through normal channels?"

She answered, "I have no Convocation orders. Nor did I seek them; I act on my own."

Luellen, sitting relaxed with arms crossed, raised his head. "You're aware that we can't allow Selenda to remain in Federation hands. We have allies up and down this arm of the galaxy, we can't allow a Federation military base right in the middle—"

She cut him off with a piercing gaze that left him, apparently, unable to speak. "There will be no military base. There will be no Rebel invasion. Both of you will allow Selenda to go on as it has for millennia, a peaceful world of no particular distinction beyond a delicious ale."

Luellen shook himself, as if making a mighty effort to throw off her spell. "What is Selenda to you?"

She looked from face to face. "Gentlemen, I am carrying out a genetic experiment on Selenda. It's been going on for over three thousand years. If you both continue on your current paths, your forces will meet here and Selenda will be devastated . . . if not destroyed altogether. The genetic material is irreplaceable. If I lose it, I shall be quite displeased." She placed her palms flat on the table and said flatly, "Perhaps you've heard legends of what happens when I am displeased. Perhaps you've heard that when Dalara Hoister stole my research, I gengineered and released upon her planet the first mosquitoes seen in two millennia. Perhaps you remember how I ruined the Talbot Kindred for what they tried on Pluvia." She took a sip of ale. "It is best that both of you leave Selenda alone."

Luellen held her gaze for long moments, then drained his flagon and wiped his mouth with the back of a hand. He laughed. "When I was a kiddo, my mother scared me with tales of the witchy wrath of Telena Hoister. I never thought I'd meet the witch in person." He stood and bowed. "If Minister

Cooke will assure me that the Federation will keep hands off Selenda, then I will agree."

Cooke lumbered to his feet, took his first sip of ale, and spat it on the ground. "That's not ale, it's piss." He frowned. "The Talbots are still paying reparations twelve hundred years along. You're a bitch, Telena. But I can't take the chance. Agreed." He turned his head. "This planet is a pesthole. Dimi, you keep your forces away and I'll have no reason to take any further interest in Selenda."

Telena stood and shook hands with both of them. "Thank you. I knew we could come to agreement. I'll be watching, of course. See that both of you behave." She sat, regarded them both. Across the square, a train glided into the station. Telena nodded in its direction. "Your ride is here. Goodbye, gentlefolk."

Cooke shook his head and turned away, striding purposefully to the station and onto the waiting train. Luellen followed, more slowly. He pointedly boarded a different car than Cooke. As the train pulled out of the station, Luellen smiled and gave a final nod. Then they were gone, solitary and invisible on a train populated by dozens.

Telena looked in my direction and, for the first time, spoke directly to me. "There, that's done. They'll keep to the agreement. Selenda is safe for now."

I bowed my head. "Your Grace, I—"

The ghost of a smile touched her lips. "Oh, don't be tedious, Erwilian. Telena is my name, please use it." She gestured to the seat Cooke had used. "Join me for another round."

Half-believing I was dreaming, I took the place at her table. She drained her flagon and wiped her mouth with the back of hand. "I don't know about you, but I'm more than a bit peckish. What's good to eat here?"

I coughed to clear my throat. "Maeve serves a dish that I'm partial to: spiced meat and vegetables wrapped in flatbread, with a warm sauce of three different cheeses for dipping."

She placed a battered coin on the table; on its face was a value of 1800 shillings, the worth of a dozen meals. "Order enough for two, and a pitcher of ale."

I beckoned a server, a comely lad with sandy hair and freckles. Telena sat back watching with seeming amusement as I ordered. The server wanded her coin and returned it showing 1670 shillings, then dashed off. In only moments, he returned with the pitcher.

I poured; Telena took a great draught and sighed. "The barley on this planet used to be dreadful, an inferior strain from Perantia. I tweaked the genome, oh, two millennia ago at least, just to make the ale minimally drinkable. But I never dreamed it could get this good. Your Maeve is a genius." She raised her flagon. "To Maeve!"

I joined in the toast, still feeling as if in a dream. The world spun about me, and not from the ale. I had never spoken with one of the Fae; they had never deigned to notice me. Yet here was this incredible woman, an ancient and terrible power who had just saved my world from destruction, sitting across from me as if it were a perfectly ordinary night at the tavern. I knew not what to say, how to behave.

The food arrived; the server lad placed the platter before me totally oblivious to Telena's presence. When he left, I showed her how to spoon meat and vegetables onto flatbread, to roll it up and dip in the cheese. She took a bite and smiled. "Delicious. Thank you, Erwilian."

I could stand no more. "H-How do you know my name?"

"I know all about you, Erwilian the Trician of Montrose. It's my business to know. I've followed your family for more than a hundred generations."

I did not doubt her for an instant. "Your—Telena, *why*? Why me? Why my family? What's so special about us?"

She chuckled. "Don't worry, we're screened. Not even the Convocation's most powerful Loops can eavesdrop." She took another bite, swallowed. "Think of it, Erwilian. Thousands and thousands of worlds like Selena, millions and millions of

Mundane villages like Montrose. It's a big galaxy, and we depend on you Mundanes. We depend on you to tend the familiars, the ones you call Sleepers, so we can use their psi abilities in our nets and Panels and Loops. We depend on your trillions of living minds to boost our own abilities. Our technology, our economy, our entire social system depend on you."

I shook my head, not understanding a quarter of what she said.

She steepled her fingers and regarded me over her slender mahogany digits. "And here on Selenda, a backwater world that never attracts any attention, a strain of Mundanes who are untouched by the Geas Ingenerate. Some odd twist of brain proteins, just the right balance of enzymes and cofactors, and you're immune to the one force keeping the whole galaxy in balance. Imagine what a tool that could be. What a weapon. What a threat. If the Convocation knew, Selenda would be cosmic dust in three minutes."

"I don't . . . ? "

She smiled. "Of course you don't. And you needn't worry. As long as I have any say in the matter, Selenda will be safe." She took another bite, grease and cheese running down her chin. With a laugh, she wiped it and licked the back of her hand. "Enough of that. Tell me of yourself, Erwilian. Tell me about your life."

"I don't know what to say." What could I possibly tell her, this woman who strode among the stars and across centuries as if in Pearce's Mead, that would be of interest?

Her eyes met mine. "Are you happy?"

I thought of Midsummer's Faire, of the Aedan teens and the power conduits, of late nights singing with friends in this very tavern, of dancing with pretty Rosetta McReigh. And I nodded. "Yes, I'm happy. Montrose is a wonderful village; I wouldn't live anywhere else for a million shillings."

For an eternal moment her eyes stayed on me, as if she were looking past skin and bone and into the very depths of my brain. Then she nodded. "Good. That's what I wanted to hear."

She gestured to the platter. "We'll split the last one." Astonished, I realized that the food was almost gone—and the pitcher down to the dregs. As she prepared the last roll, the pitcher lifted and emptied itself into our flagons. "Finish your drink, then come with me."

I stuffed the last of the food into my mouth and drained my flagon, while Telena did the same. Then she stood, her cloak swirling around her, and started walking. A bit unsteadily, I followed.

We walked back to Pearce's Mead. Telena stood straight and tall in the crimson light, looking to the west. Quietly, as if to the wind, she whispered, "Paddock calls, anon!"

In moments, the giant cat loomed once more above us. Again the ramp unrolled, right before Telena's feet. She half-turned to me and held out a hand. "Come."

Her hand was cold to the touch, but with a living warmth beneath, a core of fire sheathed in a shell of ice. Through my mind flashed old stories of the Fae, children's tales with cautions I'd paid no heed—do not accept food nor drink from them, never follow where they lead, or you are forever lost. My heart quailed at all I was leaving behind, Montrose and the tavern and Rosetta McReigh . . . but if this was my doom, then it was far too late for me already. I had surrendered to her spell, and now I had no choice but to follow her aboard her marvelous ship.

She looked at me and chuckled. "Don't be stupid. I just don't want to keep *Greymalkin* on the surface longer than necessary. I'll bring you back. When the night is done, you'll be in your own sleep cocoon wondering if you dreamed it all. But the night is far from done."

With that, she took me aboard the ship. Obsidian and gold, ruby and tawny fur, it was luxurious as a palace yet homey as my own great room. At the top of the ramp another woman stood, tall and dark and silent—lacking perhaps a shade of Telena's grace, her eyes perhaps a bit darker, but every bit as Fae. Telena gestured. "Althea Jane, one of my attendants." She addressed the woman. "High orbit, and keep us from being seen. Erwilian and I will be in my chambers. Drink and nibbly bits, nothing too heavy."

Althea Jane bowed and left; Telena looked upward and all at once we were flying, past countless decks until we came to a chamber strewn with sumptuous pillows and burbling fountains and pools of water. As we came to rest, the ceiling blossomed into a dome like the night sky, and I saw Selenda itself receding above us, blue-green and white against scattered stars, crimson highlights dancing in the oceans of the night side.

I gasped. Telena tumbled to a mound of pillows, casting her cloak aside in a swirl of midnight mist, and pulled me down next to her. "Relax, Erwilian. This is a magical night. I just saved your planet; let's celebrate a little."

Strangely, her words calmed me. Dream or reality, this *was* magic. Even if I never returned, as the old stories warned, I was here now in the company of a demigod. I might as well try to enjoy myself.

Telena gave me a tiny glass flagon, clutched in the paws of a sleek glass cat, containing a few swallows of a liquid that sparkled with iridescent color; she kept another for herself. "They call this panther dew; it's empathy-enhanced but has no lasting effect. One sip at a time, though." She raised her glass. "To Montrose!"

I answered the toast and touched the panther dew to my lips. It was like drinking a rainbow. A gentle well-being spread through my body. "That's incredible." I might be doomed, but at least I would go happily.

I don't remember half of what we talked about that night, and I understand less than a tenth of that. She told me of my distant ancestors, of the deep history of Montrose, of biological and genetic mysteries I could never comprehend. She spoke of her life and her family, and showed me images of distant worlds and other Eternal Ones with unfamiliar, majestic names. She fed me delicate and indescribable morsels of ineffable texture and flavor, each unlike the other and each like nothing I'd ever tasted. And she shared with me her own sacred body, in ecstatic agony of joy that left me both spent and triumphant.

In the end she was as good as her word. With the golden sun just creeping above the horizon, its buttery light spilling through the trees onto the sward, she had *Greymalkin* set down once again in Pearce's Mead. She walked with me to the foot of the ramp while Althea Jane stood impassively at the top.

Telena nodded toward the village. "Go home, Erwilian. Treat your Rosetta well. I expect two girls and a strapping boy."

"W-will I see you again?"

She shrugged. "Who can tell? It's an uncertain galaxy." She caught me with her eyes, those eyes in which swirled the depths of endless space. "Don't pine. Keep happiness in your heart. Be joyful until the end of your days."

I felt joy surge within me, and I knew that I would do as she said. I knew enough of energy, even then, to know that no human could long behold enormous power and live. If it happened that I never saw her again, I would still be happy.

I turned toward the village, then looked back at Telena and the great cat-shape perched above the Mead. Althea Jane looked down at her and said, "Where to now, Sayyid?"

Telena looked me up and down, then waved. "Go." She mounted the ramp. "We can shape for home now."

"You're finished here, then?"

She turned her back on me. "I have everything I came for."

The cat sprang skyward, and in the space of a single breath it was gone.

So there it is, the night that a woman from beyond the sky saved our world.

As she said, I lived happily ever on, with joy always in my heart. Rosetta and I indeed had two girls and a boy, as well as half a dozen wonderful foster children. I have many friends and am well-regarded here in Montrose. Truly, I don't miss Telena; one might as well miss the thunderstorm or the rosy dawn.

Life goes on much as it always has. We pay our tithes, foster our share of foundlings, and take our turns caring for Sleepers. We serve in the fire brigade and on the Village Council. We dance at festivals and play on ball teams, we sing in choirs, and we always lend a hand when there's a barn to raise, a house to be painted, or a child missing in the forest. In most ways, we live our lives in the age-old patterns dictated by the Eternal Ones.

But some nights, when the golden sun is gone and the ruby sun shines high in the sky, when the wind stirs the rusty turf of Pearce's Mead and I taste the pale ale that Maeve's granddaughter still makes according to the old recipe—on those nights, I look to the sky, and wonder if my children's children's children will ever witness the form of a great black cat descending once again from the stars.

I hope they will.

AUTHOR'S NOTE

My friend Elektra Hammond asked me for a story for an anthology she was putting together on the theme of spacecraft that looked like animals. As it turns out, I had a character who already tooled around in a cat-shaped ship—Telena Hoister. And I was already thinking about how to lay the groundwork for an upcoming novel to feature Telena and friends.

This story is part of the Scattered Worlds Mosaic, a whole series of novels and shorter works. If you want to find out more about Telena Hoister, her family, and her universe, check the Scattered Worlds website at *www.scatteredworlds.com.*

The Cold Solution

Menu: Shot of whiskey

Like a brisk slap to the face.

copyright © 1991, Don Sakers. Originally published in Analog, April 1991
Winner, Analog Award for Best Short Story of 1991

She wasn't alone.

There was a stowaway aboard.

She'd read a story like this once, a story so old that the original had been on paper, not wafer. All Space Force Cadets read the story – it had even been viddied a few times, but nothing could compare with the starkness of words on a bare screen. In her Academy days, they'd all stayed up late marveling at the prescience of that pre-spaceflight author, who had described it all so well.

Now it wasn't a story.

"All right, you can come out now," she said in the direction of the supply locker. "Your free ride is over." At the same time she fingered her laser knife, holding it ready in case the stowaway gave her trouble. She'd never faced one before, not in all her eleven years in the Force…but you heard stories from other pilots. Some stowaways fought, some threatened, some pleaded, some even tried to bribe you – but in the end, according to the inexorable laws of physics, all of them died.

It was sad, she supposed, in some abstract way. But Space didn't care about simple human concerns like life and death. Space was cold, and all it knew was the bottom line of its cold equations.

Self-defense, she thought. The minute her unwanted guest decided to stow away, he had sealed his fate. It was him or her. And she wasn't going to let it be her.

"Show yourself right now," she said through clenched teeth, "Or I swear, I'll shoot."

The locker door opened, and a timid voice said, "Don't shoot. I'm coming out." Then the stowaway stepped into view.

It was a boy.

The pilot closed her eyes, and for an instant she prayed, prayed to whatever gods lived out here on the edges of the explored galaxy. *When I open my eyes,* she thought, *It won't be a boy standing there, it'll be a thirty-year-old fugitive.* That was how it was *supposed* to happen.

But out here there were no gods but Space itself, and when she looked she saw only sandy hair, and freckles, and a lopsided grin flanked by a single dimple. He couldn't have been more than ten.

And no matter what she did, no matter that she wanted desperately to be anywhere in the universe but here – the boy was already dead. Despite his cheery smile and his bright eyes and his fidgeting hands, he was dead, dead as Space itself.

She lowered the laser knife and closed her jaw. "What are you doing here?"

"I'm a stowaway. I want to go to Lethe with you. My uncle Matt works there." The boy said it so simply, as if it were a self-evident geometrical axiom. "I know I wasn't supposed to, but I haven't seen him for a long time."

"How old are you?"

"Nine."

"Do your parents – " She stopped herself, knowing only too late what his answer must be.

The boy shook his head. "They don't know I'm here." He glanced at his watch. "They're probably still asleep, back on the ship." Cocking his head at Diane, he asked, "How come you launched in the middle of the night?"

He knew nothing, she realized, of the inexorable mathematics of celestial mechanics – the mathematics which had already killed him. "Th-the launch window was just twenty minutes wide," she said, not caring whether her words meant anything to him. "There's only one optimal trajectory to Lethe tangent to the ship's flight path." And now, she thought, the ship was back in hyperspace...beyond contact until it reached its destination. The lad's parents wouldn't hear the news of their son's fate until two weeks from now, when the ship burst out of translight in the Gondwana system. Two weeks too late....

"How did you know I was going to Lethe? What made you think of stowing away?"

The boy thrust out his chest and beamed. "Technician Godwin told me. We're good friends."

"Do you know *why* I'm headed there?"

Another nod. "Medicine. For the plague. We were worried when we heard about it on the news. With Uncle Matt there, and everything." Incredibly, he was still smiling. "But now everything's going to be all right, isn't it?"

"Wait. Don't move." Diane closed her eyes, leaned her head back on the command chair, and concentrated. From the million tiny pinpricks of the nerve inducers, she felt the computer's cool, quiet presence in the intricate neural lattices that filled the whole structure of the boat. Without a pilot's living brain in the circuit, it was no more intelligent than a wrist chronometer. But when joined to the implants in Diane's brain tissue, the computer could easily handle the millions of picosecond calculations of close approach, effortlessly direct the boat's thrusters to ensure a safe entry and touchdown.

Pilot and computer, each incomplete without the other – and together, more powerful than both.

But not powerful enough.

In answer to her unasked question, Diane felt the numbers within her mind. The boat was 31.62 kilograms over-massed, and therefore using an extra six grams of fuel per second, each second of deceleration. It might as well have been sixty grams a second, or six thousand...the boat would arrive at Lethe some seventy kilograms of fuel short. And then it would burn up, a splendid meteor trail in Lethe's nighttime sky.

Damned if it *will*, Diane thought.

The kid twitched. "Look, I know I wasn't supposed to stow away. I'm sorry, and I'll take whatever punishment I've got coming."

"Do you know what's going to happen to you?"

"I'll have to stay on Lethe until the next ship comes. And that'll be months. I know. I'll stay with Uncle Mark. Do you know him? Mark Sadako, he works in the Colony Survey office."

Diane shrugged. "I don't think so. This is only my third trip to Lethe." And probably my last, she finished to herself. The regulations say this kid has to die – but I'm still going to get buried for it.

"He's a nice man. Look, if there's any kind of fine or something, Uncle Mark will take care of it. Or my Dad. He has *lots* of money."

There's not enough money in the universe, kid, to change the laws of physics.

Why couldn't it have been a fugitive, or transportee, or even some terrorist on a mission from God? Gods of all heaven, why did it have to be an innocent little boy?

She turned to the control board, at the same time framing a command in her mind. The computer obediently opened a hyperwave comm channel. "Lethe Port here." The voice filled the tiny cabin. "Identification, please."

"DelMinna, Boat 378H7. Get me the Base Commander."

"Why – "

"This is an emergency. I want your commander on the line, and I want him *now*."

"Hold on." Diane had to give Lethe Port credit; in less than a minute another voice, this one deeper and more controlled, said, "Commander Barker here. What's your situation?"

Diane took a breath. "Commander, I'm about seven hours out from Lethe..."

"Is the medicine all right?"

"Yes. It's not that." She took a breath. "The problem is, Commander, I've discovered a stowaway."

"Is that all?" A patronizing tone crept into the Commander's voice. "Let me look at your telemetry...hmm, pretty tight on that fuel reserve. You're thirty-two kilos over. You'd better jettison within the hour, or you'll be short for landing."

"That's the thing, Commander. This isn't an ordinary stowaway."

"I don't care *who* it is, Pilot, that medicine has *got* to get here safely. I want you to – "

"Commander, he's a little boy."

"What?!"

Carefully, slowly, Diane replied, "Commander, my stowaway is a nine-year-old boy. He didn't know what he was doing." She bit the words off savagely. "One of your ColSurv people is the boy's uncle. The kid just wanted to see him."

All trace of patronizing was gone from the Commander's voice. "Stand by, Pilot. We'll get our people to work on it."

"Commander...the kid is right here, watching me. What should I tell him."

There was a long pause, then in a tone laced with infinite regret, the Commander replied, "Tell him the truth."

"What's your name, kid?"

"Tony." The boy hung his head like a puppy caught making a mess in the house.

Diane's brain had gone on vacation, leaving her vocal chords to figure out what to say all on their own. What *was* there to say? No perfect words had ever been invented for this situation. "Tony, you have to understand something." Why was it important that he understand? Why couldn't she just slug the kid, knock him unconscious, throw him in the airlock and be done with it?

Because she had to live with herself afterward.

"Tony, the payload of an emergency boat like this has to be carefully figured. Every gram counts. That's why emergency boat pilots are usually women. But when they fueled the boat, they didn't figure on your extra mass. Do you understand that?"

Tony nodded, but kept his eyes down. "I guess we're using more fuel than you planned. I'm sorry about that."

Sorry isn't enough. "That's the thing, Tony. The people on Lethe have their big computers working on this, but right now...well, it looks like we're going to run out of fuel before we get there. We won't have enough to land safely."

Tony raised his head, and his eyes were dry. Diane wondered how long they'd stay that way. "Why didn't they give you more fuel?"

"Everything is calculated. The ship doesn't have much fuel to spare – and every extra gram of fuel meant at least one less gram of medicine for Lethe." She wanted to turn away from his accusing stare, wanted to shout, "It's not my fault!" Instead, she forced herself to meet his eyes.

"S-so I guess you have to jettison something. That's what the Commander said, isn't it? You'll have to throw something overboard, to make up for my mass. Geez, I'm sorry."

"Tony, we – " The chime of the hyperwave interrupted her.

"Boat 378H7, this is Commander Barker. Look, DelMinna, our computers have looked at the problem, and they have some recommendations for you. Number one: you'll approach Lethe on an orbit that's a bit more shallow, so you can pick up some extra delta-vee by skimming off the atmosphere. Number two: Your landing site will be changed to a splashdown in the inland sea; one of our helicopters will pick up you and the medicine."

"And what does that get me?"

"You're still twenty-five kilos overmass. And your approach will hit five gees. But you won't have to do a jettison until seventy-three minutes before splashdown."

An hour and a quarter short.

Might as well be a year.

Hey kid, Diane thought, can you hold your breath for seventy-three minutes? Can you flap like a bird and make atmosphere entry safely?

She swallowed. "Is that all you can do for me?"

"That's all the computers can come up with. What did you have in mind?"

"I don't know." Refueling? Don't be stupid, Diane. You're falling toward Lethe at better than two hundred kilometers a second. What are you going to do when a fuel rocket goes past – reach out and grab it with a butterfly net? "Jettison at seventy-three minutes before touchdown, eh?"

"That's the best we can do for you, Pilot."

"Thanks. Out." Bitterly, she commanded the computer to cut the link. As it did, the machine signaled seven hours until touchdown.

Tony had five and three-quarter hours to live.

Diane opened her mouth, then closed it. The words wouldn't come – she doubted that there *were* words.

Tony looked around the small cabin. A single glance sufficed. Control chair and board, airlock, cargo cupboard with its load of medicine, broom-closet supply locker…that was all. "When it comes time, what are we going to throw out?"

Diane couldn't make herself be cruel enough to do the kind thing, and tell the kid right away. She stalled. "There isn't much here to get rid of." Please, gods, let him at least figure it out for himself, so she could be spared pronouncing the sentence of death.

"It doesn't look like there's *anything*. I guess you'll toss out food and water – "

"There isn't any food aboard, Tony. Only a couple of liters of water."

"And you can't throw out the medicine." He looked again, more carefully, and his eyes grew wider. "The locker doors are welded on, so is that couch you're sitting in."

"The control couch is part of the navigation system. Even if I *could* rip it out, the ship can't land without it."

"Your pressure suit?"

"There isn't one aboard." She waved at her jumpsuit. "All I have is what you see."

"Then what are you going to jettison?"

She couldn't delay the awful moment any longer. "Tony... the regulations say that any stowaway must be jettisoned." She noticed that her knuckles were white on the grip of her knife, and forced her hand to relax.

For a moment, Tony's expression was unchanged – then all too quickly, the lad of ten grew up, and cold terror entered his eyes. "I-If I leave the ship, I'll *die*."

"Tony, there's no other way."

"You can't do that." Tony backed up a step, found himself pressed against the airlock's inner door, and moved sideways to the supply locker. "I haven't done anything to die for."

"I know. I'm sorry." Her heart thudded, and each breath was agony. "I-I wish I could take your place. But don't you see, you couldn't pilot the ship. The computer needs a trained pilot in the couch. I'd just be killing both of us – and all the people on Lethe who need the serum."

"There's got to be *something* we can do."

She shook her head. "You heard Lethe Port. Even using our full fuel reserve, we're twenty-five kilos overmass."

"I weigh thirty-one." The boy plucked at his shirt, garish red and orange synthetic. "If we get rid of our clothes, and our shoes, and the couple of liters of water...and if we could cut these doors loose..."

Diane shook her head. "Five kilos, maybe. Not enough."

"Can't we go into orbit, and wait for another ship to come get us?"

"Tony, Lethe's a new colony. They don't *have* any ships. That's why we have to send an emergency boat."

"Isn't there *anything* that anybody can do for me?"

She closed her eyes. "No. Nothing."

"Do you want me to die?"

The question was so innocent, asked in such a gentle tone, that it finally broke Diane's reserve. Her eyes filled as she reached out her arms to the helpless little boy. "Of course not. I don't want it to happen." He fell into her arms and she squeezed him tightly. His sobs shook both their bodies. "Nobody wants it. But space doesn't have any feeling, Tony. Physics doesn't care what we *want*."

Tony was silent, then, quaking with quiet sobs. Diane held on, and sobbed along with him.

The boy asked to use the control keyboard to write a letter to his parents. Diane gave him the control couch and busied herself counting the vials of serum in the cargo compartment. When that palled, she leaned against the wall and stared at the airlock, thinking.

Clothes and water, five kilos. They could each shield some vials with their bodies, throwing out some packing material – another kilo or two. If they both emptied their bladders…

No good. She sniffed, noticing that the air was already a little stale. The recycler was calibrated for one occupant only.

Air! Trying not to show any eagerness – for to give Tony any false hope at this stage would be viciously cruel – she calculated mentally. The airlock had a volume of about three cubic meters, if she disabled the pumps and dumped an airlock-full at a time into space, reduced the pressure by a quarter, maybe a third –

In spite of herself, she sighed. At most, dumping the air would only get her a kilo or two. Still nowhere near enough.

Diane put her head back against the wall and closed her eyes. There was nothing to do, nothing at all. Tony's fate was sealed, sealed by the cold equations of nature, and nothing human had any power to stop it. Maybe, she thought, we don't belong out here at all. Maybe we should have stayed on Earth

and minded our own business. Then there wouldn't be any
colonies, no ships, no emergency boats.

And no little boys would have to die.

But little boys died all the time, even on Earth, died in
accidents, died of horrible diseases that wasted them away to
nothing, died of hunger and neglect, were murdered...little
boys had always died, as long as there *were* little boys, and
nothing was ever going to change that fact. Wishing, no matter
how desperately, would not change the universe's cold
equations one bit.

The gentle buzz of the computer's alert signal pulled Diane
to full consciousness. Had she slept? Apparently, for when she
glanced at the chronometer she saw that they were two hours
away from landing.

Tony was awake, too, his eyes intent upon her as he gave
up the command couch and allowed her to settle her head
within the computer's contacts. She didn't know if he, too, had
slept...and she realized it was not her business how he'd spent
his last hours.

"Is it time?"

"Almost," Diane said. "Just over 45 minutes left."

"You're going to have a hard landing, aren't you? Because
of me."

"It's nothing worse than what I went through at the
Academy," she lied.

"But the medicine will be all right, won't it?" He glanced
back at the cargo compartment. "It's important to me, that the
medicine gets there okay. I'd hate...I'd hate to die for nothing."

Diane nodded. "I'll make sure it gets there safely."

Tony lowered his eyes. "I-If I go now, you'll have a little
extra fuel. Just in case something happens."

She didn't know how to answer him.

"I...I want to say thank you. You've been good to me. I
know that there's no other way, and I know you'd do
something to help me if you could." He raised his chin and
stepped toward the airlock. "I'd like to do it now, please."

"Tony." He kept his back to her, didn't see her outstretched hand. He faced the airlock, and the cold bitterness of space beyond, with his head high and his shoulders square.

And the gods of space, she thought, would have one more sacrificial victim, one more life to prove that their word was law. They weren't cruel or vindictive, they weren't even gods at all – just impassionate Nature, her will expressed in the frozen lattice of her cold equations.

Damn it, Diane thought, it isn't Humanity's way to give up and yield to impossibilities. There was something within the human animal, something which wanted to fight back. She'd known that ever since she'd read that oh-so-prophetic story, had known it when her heart protested, *there has to be a way*.

"Will you open the door, please?"

"Tony," she repeated, "I want you to know that I wish I could do something to save you. I don't like this any more than you do." Except you won't have to live with the guilt for the rest of your life. "I'd give anything to stop this from happening. I'd give…anything."

In that moment, her mind was made up, and she knew what she must do. Just as good that he had his back to her, for if she saw his eyes, she would never be able to act.

Quickly, silently, she raised her laser knife, dialed the beam to maximum, and thumbed the button home. A ruby-red beam lanced forth, filling the cabin with an eerie, bloody light.

"Pilot DelMinna? Pilot, can you hear me?"

Diane opened her eyes on a hospital room. She was in bed, wired to a dozen instruments, and a bearded face was looking down at her. She'd seen him before…yes, the Lethe Base Commander. "Are you awake?"

"Yes," she croaked. "But I wish I wasn't."

"I can understand. You've been under sedation…and hypnotherapy…for six days." He touched her shoulder. "The Space Force top brass want to speak to you on the hyperwave.

There are commendations to be given and medals to be awarded, and I'm sure they want to put you through the worst debriefing in history. I told them they can't have you until you feel up to it."

"Thank you." Something rumbled in her gut, and she turned her head away. When the feeling passed, she looked back at the Commander. "The serum…?"

"The serum survived your landing beautifully, and it's been distributed throughout the colony. MedCorps says the plague is under control. You're a hero, DelMinna. In more ways than one."

"Yeah." She sighed. "What about Tony?"

"The boy is safe and sound, not three doors down from here." He smiled. "You can see him, if you wish."

"I don't know. He might not want to see me."

"He's asked for you."

Diane shivered. "How will he be?"

"I should let his doctor answer that – but I can give you an outline. They say that he's young enough for regeneration treatments to take. In another year or two, he'll grow back that arm, and both legs. In two years, they swear he'll never even know they were gone."

Before her mind's eye flashed the memory of that horrible instant when the laser beam connected, the awful smell and Tony's scream.

"You did the right thing, Pilot." The Commander gripped her shoulder firmly. "Your laser cauterized the wound instantly. The computer records that you started approach to Lethe a good two kilos under maximum mass. Good thinking."

She was afraid to lift her sheet, afraid to look…but she had to know. "And me…?"

The Commander's face clouded. "Regeneration isn't an exact science. After a certain age, the cells lose their ability to… that is, the medical team tried everything they could think of…"

She covered his hand with her own. "Don't worry," she said, nodding. "I'm not sorry for what I did. I can live with it." She forced a smile. "After all, it's not like I live and work under gravity." She shrugged. "What does a Pilot need legs for, after all?" If she said it enough times, she thought, she'd even start to believe it.

"In your case, they came in handy," he grunted. Then, under the pretense of covering a nervous cough, he took his hand away from hers. "DelMinna, you're going to be the talk of the Space Force for this little trick. You're the only Pilot who's ever figured out how to beat the Cold Equations scenario. What made you think of it?"

"Something I almost said to Tony, at the last minute." In imagination, she was back in the cabin, and she knew that a part of her would always be there. "I told him that I'd give anything to avoid throwing him out the airlock." She gave a chuckle that wasn't entirely forced. "I almost said: *I'd give my right arm to stop this from happening.*" She shrugged. "After that, it was simple."

Simple. So why would it haunt her for the rest of her life?

Because Nature doesn't suffer her defeats gladly, she thought. *And there's always a price to be paid.*

"Would you like to see the lad now?" The Commander stepped back. "Orderlies are ready to help you."

Diane closed her eyes, and looked again on her moment of truth. *I'll pay the price*, she thought, *And gladly. That's part of being human.*

She opened her eyes and nodded. "I'd like that very much."

AUTHOR'S NOTE

Like everyone else, I cried at the end of Tom Godwin's story "The Cold Equations." Godwin's story is deservedly a classic, and the unforgettable point it makes—that natural laws have no respect for emotion, and that sometimes the little girl has to go out the airlock—was well-needed as a counter to the school of SF that said it was always possible to come up with a new force, ray, or vibration that could save the day. (Kipling was probably making a similar point when he wrote "The Gods of the Copybook Headings," but that's a discussion for another day.)

Godwin's point was also quite consistent with the mechanistic, male-based, rigorous-logic science of the day. Ultimately, the universe was a cold and heartless place, and unless you obeyed its rules, it would kill you as soon as look at you.

While I grasped the point, I didn't buy it for a second.

By the time I was writing, the world was a different place. Newtonian mechanics was replaced by quantum mechanics. The Uncertainty Principle was well-understood. And male engineers no longer dominated the field of SF.

The old logic said that there was no escape from the Cold Equations scenario. There were only two choices: either the girl died, or the colonists perished. Either way, someone was dead. All that remained was to do the math and pick the option with the fewest corpses.

That's one way to look at the world. It's a hierarchical, rules-based, binary-logic way...without getting into too many labels, a stereotypically-male way.

Another way of looking at the world is a networked, exceptions-based, fuzzy-logic way...if you will, a stereotypically-female way. And that way said that there *had* to be a solution that saved everyone.

[I don't really believe that all women think that way, nor that all men think the other way. But as a fiction writer I deal in symbolism, and here the symbolism is vital. Let's say that there's the M way and the F way, and each of us has some degree of M and F inside, and leave discussions of gender to another venue.]

After that, it was just a matter of finding a solution—in this case, remembering that you didn't have to put the whole stowaway out the airlock, just the same mass in body parts. There are other solutions to the Cold Equations scenario. I leave it as an exercise to the student to find them (although if anyone wants to do an anthology of such stories, let me know!)

Once I started on the story, I realized that I had to make the pilot a woman. Look, I was saying to the SF world, when you make the pilot a woman, it changes *everything*. I considered leaving the stowaway a little girl, but decided to make him a boy in the interest of symmetry.

The important point is not any given solution to this particular scenario...it's something larger, just as Godwin's point was something larger. Just as SF once needed to hear that there were times when the girl had to go out of the airlock, in 1991 SF needed to hear that the girl didn't *always* have to go out the airlock. That there are two ways of looking at the world, and both of them are valid and necessary.

This story was a favorite of the *Analog* readership. It won the award for Best Short Story in the year it was published.

The Slow Train

Menu: Darjeeling and scones with clotted cream

So very British.

copyright © 2004, Don Sakers. Originally published in Analog, October 2004

Susan Shetland awoke to the far-off call of a train whistle.

She smiled, lingering in the wake of pleasant dreams, then gave a languid stretch and glanced at the clock. Half past seven. Time to get up.

Susan gave her sleeping husband a final glance, then made her way downstairs for breakfast. It was a typically chilly English morning, and the wind had a tendency to whistle right through the walls and windows of Uncle George's old house.

The stout housekeeper was reading a romance paperback by the fire when Susan descended the steep, creaky stairs. "No, don't get up, Emma. You look so comfortable. I'll make my own breakfast."

"Bless you, dear, but it's no bother." The older woman steered Susan to the table. "You just sit down right here and have a cuppa to take the chill off." Steaming tea appeared as if by magic. "I'll be right back with some warm oatmeal and some eggs for you, just as you like them."

Stirring her tea, Susan sighed. Uncle George was so seldom home that the poor old woman was alone in the house most of the time; Emma had told Susan that she thoroughly enjoyed these two weeks with, as she put it, "someone to care for again."

She sipped, allowing the tea and the fire to warm her.

Two weeks. And it had been marvelous. She'd been away from England for far too long, and when Uncle George had offered them plane tickets and a month's use of his country house, she'd jumped at the chance.

Maybe that was my mistake, she thought. I should have asked Bob before I accepted. But who would have thought that he'd have any objections to a free month in Britain?

Not that his objections had been sensible, any of them. Neither of them had any trouble scheduling vacation time from work, and it was easy enough for his parents to take care of the apartment while they were gone. He seemed to be against the holiday, simply for the sole reason that she wanted it.

She drained her cup and poured another from the ancient teapot beneath its quilted cozy. Lately, Bob had been objecting to too many things, and all for the same lack of reasons. If she said it was night, he would insist that the sun was up.

Well, damn if she was going to let his foul moods affect her good time! She had lived without him for—

The front door opened, and Uncle George stepped in. And Susan felt her heart lift as if she were a little girl again and he was arriving unannounced at the family's tiny flat with an armload of gifts and treats.

"Glory be, the Master's home," cried Emma, racing for the chubby, silver-haired gentleman in his ridiculous pseudo-Victorian suit and coat. George Merrick lifted her for a moment by the elbows, then spun her around and deposited her again on the floor.

"Lord, but it's good to be welcomed to a nice warm home on a day like this," he said in a resonant baritone. "Emma, get some hot food on that table, and keep it coming! Susan, love, come here and say hello to your Uncle."

Laughing, Susan threw her arms around him and gave him a quick peck on the cheek. "I didn't know you were coming. I'd have made sure everything was ready."

"Not to worry. Business, don't you know? I'd have been here two days ago if it weren't for business." His eyes lighted on the table. "Is that tea I see? I've spent half the night driving from London, my toes are frozen." Shedding his outerwear, he marched to the table and plopped in a chair. Susan poured for him, then took up her own cup.

"We've been having a tremendous time here, Uncle. I can't thank you enough for letting us use the place."

Chuckling, he waved her thanks aside. "Not at all, not at all. This poor old house sits lonely most of the time, but can't bear to part with it. Been in the family forever, you know. Wish you two could come live here year-round."

Stunned, Susan gave a nervous chuckle. "So do I!" Was he serious? Would he really turn the place over to her and Bob, just like that? She'd known that Uncle George was rich, but she'd had no idea….

Emma came in with a heaping plate of eggs, bacon, steaming oatmeal, and the curiously English brown-on-one-side toast. "There's more where this came from," she said as she set the plate in front of George.

Susan helped herself to a portion about twice the size of her usual breakfast—when she got home, she was going to have to do some serious dieting—then watched in amazement as Uncle George proceeded to finish off the rest of the ample platter. Working like a power digger, he kept shoveling it in; and all the while he kept up a fast-running conversation with both Susan and Emma. How on earth did he manage it?

When at last the plates were clean and the last of the tea poured, Susan leaned back and regarded the old man over the rim of her cup. "Uncle, you didn't spend the night driving from London just to see Bob and me. Something else brought you out here."

His feigned expression of surprise melted into a smile. "I could never fool you, even when you were a little girl." He glanced at the window, where rosy dawnlight spilling through lace curtains made intricate spiderwebs of light on the wall. "My dear, how would you like to go for a drive?"

Susan hesitated only an instant, thinking of Bob still asleep upstairs. Then she pushed her chair back from the table and stood, forcing him out of her mind. "I'd love to."

Uncle George's Rolls was one of the new electric models; it purred silently as he guided it down the lane, into the village, and around the roundabout with the unconscious skill of a native. Susan, used to driving American highways in her perky little diesel Rabbit, was still cautious about English roads…and absolutely terrified of the roundabout.

Soon, though, they were beyond the village and out on open road. Morning mist lay low on the countryside as if daring the sun to do something about it. Susan leaned back in her seat with a contented sigh. Before she moved to the States, she and Uncle George had often gone on impromptu trips like this, driving from one end of Dorset to the other in search of Thomas Hardy's great-grandfather's cottage, the village that Viscount Milton moved, or the exact spot where Louisa Musgrove fell.

She'd tried to interest Bob in making such an excursion during this vacation, but he was far too intent upon watching English television and seeing the usual tourist sights: Stonehenge, Stratford, Bath. In the end she gave up, settling instead for long strolls alone through the surrounding countryside, or evenings at the local pub with the townsfolk.

She and Bob had been growing apart for quite a while now. At first she'd made efforts to close the gap; but as years went on, the attempt was not worth the effort. Bob wanted to make money; his career and his bank account were the most important things in his life. Sometimes Susan wished she could win the lottery; she would give Bob all the money so that the two of them could get on with their lives.

She had to give him credit: at least he had come along to England. Perhaps he wanted to heal the rift as much as she did …but neither of them knew the way.

Whistling, Uncle George drove the car onward, following its shadow up one hill and down another toward the West

Country. Susan started; had she fallen asleep? The sun seemed higher, the morning less chilly. "Where are we going, Uncle?"

He grinned. "You'll see when we get there." For a moment he was silent, then he said, "Tell me, have you lost your fascination with trains?"

"Oh, no!" she blurted at once. "Of course, there's not much opportunity for train-spotting in the States." And with work, she added to herself, and the apartment, and Bob, she hadn't had a chance to ride a train for …years. Bob didn't like the train; he said it was too slow. Their few long trips had been by plane. "It's been too long."

He smiled. "Good, then. You're in for a treat."

"We're going to see a train?"

A chuckle. "You'll know when we get there. No more questions, now."

When Uncle George said "no more questions," he meant no more questions. He was intent upon a surprise, and she would have to wait for it. She turned her attention back to the unfolding landscape outside, and to watching the road signs.

Faded and rusted, overgrown with hardy weeds or standing slightly askew on posts of dark, weathered wood, the signs called to her with names of nearby villages and towns: Milton Abbas, Ansty Cross, Corscombe, Netherbury, Monkton Wyld, and a dozen others, each more evocative than the last. Nowhere else in the world, she thought, would you find place names such as the English had. She loved each and every one of them.

The car topped another hill and headed downward. Spread out before her was a broad valley of such lush green that it nearly made Susan gasp at the sight. A narrow stream flowed through the valley, and a cluster of tumbledown buildings in the middle distance neatly straddled the water. Uncle George slowed the car, and Susan knew that their destination was ahead.

"Where are we?" she asked.

"That's Coombe-on-Axe," he answered, gesturing at the village. "I would be surprised if anyone lives here now, but in its day it was quite a pleasant town." He glanced her way with a smile. "I understand that the pub had the friendliest landlord and heartiest beer in West Dorset."

Susan chuckled. "Both would have to be outstanding to beat The Queen's Carriage."

"What a pity the establishment is no longer in business, so we can't compare." Two or three miles outside the town, the paved road suddenly became a dirt track. Uncle George eased the car to the side and shut off the engine. "I'm afraid we'll have to walk the rest of the way. I hope you don't mind."

"When did I ever mind walking with you?"

Susan stepped out into the sunlight and stretched. She took a deep breath; the air was clean, fresh, and cool, and it carried the barely-perceptible scent of honeysuckle. She thought she could hear the distant rush of the stream.

Opening the trunk, Uncle George assembled a two-wheeled luggage cart and piled a few battered leather suitcases upon it. Then he took the handle and started toward the town. "Come along."

Susan took the cart from him. "Are you going somewhere?"

"All in good time, dear. For the moment, let's enjoy the stroll."

Enjoy it she did. Although Uncle George glanced at his watch once or twice, he did not seem to be in any particular hurry, and the dirt lane was a pleasant succession of one magnificent view after another. Susan lost track of time, but she supposed they had strolled a good half hour before they came into town.

If anyone did still live here, Susan didn't know where they might be; the houses and shops were boarded up and their lawns choked with ivy, tall grass, and a few brave saplings. Even the street was impassable with fallen branches, great potholes, and one puddle so huge that she thought it could better be called a pond. Nobody, Susan suspected, had been here for two dozen years…at least.

Still, Uncle George led the way as if he knew where he was going. They walked down a slow incline toward the stream, then turned onto a side street and away from the village. Before the houses came to an end, though, the ruin of a train station appeared around a bend.

If the town had seen better days, Susan thought, then the station had forgotten them. It was a long, low building whose crimson brick was dark with the dirt and dust of a hundred years. A corner of the roof was caved in, and a large oak tree grew right through the back wall.

The tracks beyond were rusted and all but lost in tall yellow grass. No train had been by here, probably, in her lifetime. Susan looked a quizzical smile at her uncle. "I hope we're not waiting for the local, because it's going to be a long wait."

He glanced at his watch and then slipped it back into his vest. "Another half hour, if that. Not that long at all." Then he stepped around the corner out of her sight.

This was so like him, she thought. Yet she couldn't be annoyed. He was preparing to spring some surprise, and knowing him it would be something wonderful. Braced for a start, she turned the corner and gasped.

The front of the station was as tumbled-down as the back: the wooden platform was half-collapsed, half overgrown with ivy, decades of rain had washed a gully beneath the tracks, and the once-shingled roof gaped open to admit the morning sun.

And standing amid all this ruin was a Victorian tea party that would have done Lewis Carroll proud.

Nearly two dozen men and women stood on the slanting platform, all dressed in the finery of a bygone day. The men wore top hats and high collars, the women bustles and vast expanses of crinoline. A few small children in tee shirts and jeans seemed completely out of place. A railway luggage cart, piled high with trunks and suitcases, sat next to the tracks beyond the platform.

Most of the people were elderly, but a few couples (the ones who belonged to the children?) seemed to be roughly Susan's age. All, no matter what their age, stood with eyes fixed on the tracks—exactly, Susan thought with rising unease, as if they were waiting for a train.

"Uncle George—"

A nearby man turned in her direction, smiled, and extended a hand to Uncle George. "George! Good to see you, old man. Wondered if you would make it this time."

"Hello, Harry. Wouldn't miss it for the world, you know." He gestured to Susan. "Miss Shetland, my...niece. Susan, this is Harry Templeton." Uncle George rocked back on his heels for a moment. "Quite a gathering. Larger than last time."

"Oh, you missed Sherborne in '53. Must have been half a hundred of them. An' a good six-and-twenty boarded that day. Don't suppose we'll see another like that."

"Not for a long while."

"That's for sure." Harry Templeton narrowed his eyes. "You're boarding today, George?"

"Aye."

"And your...niece?" He nodded toward Susan.

"She...er...hasn't made up her mind yet." Uncle George tipped his hat. "Have to go put my bags on the stack, Harry. Talk to you later."

"Of course. Once we're aboard."

Susan tried not to stare dumbly as Uncle George took her hand and pulled her toward the luggage cart. The others seemed to be ignoring them as she lifted his small bags onto the heap already there.

"Uncle, what's going on here? It's some kind of anniversary, I can tell that...but anniversary of what?" What could possibly bring all these people—in costume—out here into the middle of nowhere to stand on a deserted train platform (with their luggage, no less) and pretend that a train was coming down rails that had not seen an engine for thirty years or more?

"Child," Uncle George began softly, "I don't quite know how to tell you all this. To begin with, I'm not your great-uncle as you believe."

Best, she decided, to humor him. "All right, then, who are you?"

"If I've counted right—and I think I have—then I'm your great-great-grandfather."

Before she could react, before she could even think to be shocked or to laugh or to fall down screaming into a puddle on the ground, Susan heard a sound that cut through the still morning air and shot directly into her heart, paralyzing her. It was a sound that couldn't possibly be, yet it was so close and so loud that she knew she could not be mistaken.

Clear and strong, an approaching train whistle split the air.

Susan had never fainted before, had never known anyone who fainted. Consequently, she was surprised to find herself on the ground, looking up at a circle of half a dozen concerned faces.

She struggled to sit up, and found Uncle George's strong arms supporting her. He looked a little sheepish. "Susan, my dear, I am so sorry. I should have told you earlier."

She sat up. "I-I think I'm all right." The others stepped away, politely giving Susan and her uncle a measure of privacy. "Unc—" She stopped, then started again, "George, you can't be my great-great grandfather. That would make you over a hundred years old."

"One hundred eighty-six last April, to be precise." His look of distress grew more acute. "Oh, dear, I'm doing this so badly."

"What's going on here? What was that whistle? There can't really be a train coming…can there?"

"Take a look."

She looked down the tracks, and for a moment she saw nothing. But no...there it was. The barest outline, only just visible over trees and distant hills, like the first instant of image in a polaroid photograph: an old-time steam locomotive drawing an indistinct column of passenger cars. Susan blinked, and it was gone; blinked again, and she was surprised she could miss it. Motionless, the engine very definitely loomed as if it had been frozen in the process of steaming into the station.

A plump, kind-faced woman stepped over and crouched next to Susan and offered her a paper cup. "Here, dear, I thought you might want some water. It's something of a shock, isn't it?"

"Thank you." She drank thirstily. "Frankly, I don't have the slightest idea what's going on."

The woman frowned at George. "Never knew a man to do a good job of explaining anything," she said. "Here, let me help you up." One broad arm levered Susan to her feet. "I am Mrs. Gladstone; you must call me Maggie."

"Susan."

"Please to meet you, Susan. Oh, let me see if I can clear up your confusion. George, what have you told her so far?"

Uncle George seemed a little put out. "Only that I'm her great-great grandfather. I was doing fine until—"

"Pish-tosh. Susan, have you ever heard of the Slow Train?"

"You mean the milk train?"

Maggie smiled. "No, not quite. I don't suppose you've read Mr. H. G. Wells' *When the Sleeper Wakes*?"

"I read *War of the Worlds* in high school."

"No, I'm afraid...ah, well, certainly you've heard of Rip Van Winkle?"

"Of course."

"In Mr. Irving's story, Mr. Winkle fell asleep for a hundred years. The Slow Train...well, the Slow Train does the same thing. It left London in the 1830's, and it's been chugging along ever since then at about a mile a year. Of course, on board time moves much more slowly. One minute on the Slow Train is nearly two months on the outside."

Susan shook her head. "That's incredible." She glanced down the tracks, uneasily aware that the ghostly engine was rather more distinct than it had been only a minute ago. "Impossible. We can't even do something like that today—in 1830 they couldn't have…."

Maggie nodded, patting Susan's hand. "I can't pretend to understand Professor Möbius' mathematics. I don't think anyone can understand his theories. And his marvelous Time-Distortion Engine is certainly the most complicated machine I've ever seen. All I know is that it *does* work."

The woman was so earnest, Susan found her self starting to believe. She looked at George. "Were you aboard when the train started?"

He nodded, a faraway look in his eye. "I had lost my wife two years before. My sons were moved out; there was nothing to hold me." He sighed. "When the train stopped at Milton-on-Stour in 1928, I hopped off to see the wonderful world of the future. I'd left a few investments, which had grown in the last century, and I was able to set myself up a good business. Originally, I only intended to stay until the next scheduled stop in 1953—but in the interim, I found my family."

"Mother…."

"Yes. Your mother was my great-granddaughter; the last child of my line. I introduced myself to her as a long-lost uncle. She and your father took me into their hearts and made me feel quite at home." He shrugged. "When you were born, I knew I couldn't bear to leave you until you were grown." He looked away. "I wish your mother and father had lived to see you as you are now. They would be so proud."

"Mother always thought you were the greatest," Susan said. Oh, that sounded so inadequate. "So did I."

George smiled. "Thank you. She always made me feel like I belonged. When the Slow Train stopped again in 1975 I attended in order to see old friends I hadn't spoken with for almost fifty years. But I wasn't at all tempted to re-board."

"I'm glad you didn't." Susan glanced at the Train, which by now was a definite presence. She could no longer see the sky through its black iron bulk. "And today...?"

He shrugged. "I'm an old man. And the next scheduled stop is more than twenty years from now. I'll never make it."

"Are there ever...unscheduled stops?"

Maggie answered instantly, "Just once. During the Second World War. We all thought the world was coming to an end. But Mr. Bergenfeld—he's our Engineer—got the Train running again."

"Then..." Susan took George's hand. "Then you'll be going."

He nodded. "The train will stay in this station for about an hour. After that it's 'All aboard!' and goodbye to this world for twenty years."

The whistle sounded again, this time louder and more exuberant. Maggie smiled. "Andrew—Mr. Bergenfeld—has an extra-low-frequency whistle that sounds just fine in the outside world. He loves to blow it." She looked off into the distance. "Sometimes along the Slow Train's route, you'll hear that whistle when it looks like there's no train around for miles."

Before Susan could answer, or even think what to say, there was a tremendous roar coupled with a frantic, ear-splitting hiss. The Train, which so far had been nearly motionless, lurched forward, erupting into complete solidity. The air was filled with the screech of brakes and billowing clouds of white steam. All heads turned, all eyes captive of the tremendous spectacle. Belching steam and spitting fire, the giant black behemoth screeched to a stop with an effort that shook the entire station.

The Slow Train had arrived.

Susan moved as if in a dream. Maybe she *was* dreaming, she thought. Maybe she still slept in the big bed in Uncle George's house, huddled away from Bob and the cold and just dreaming of the Slow Train.

If so, she wasn't sure she wanted to awaken.

George helped her onto the Train with an oddly archaic grace, a Victorian gentleman giving his arm to a lady. Then, he introduced her to the Engineer, and gave her a tour of the Slow Train.

It all looked like something out of Jules Verne or Sherlock Holmes: the elegant dining car with its starched tablecloths and fresh-cut flowers, the plush upholstery of the passenger coaches, the smart, pseudo-military uniforms of the porters and conductor. And the people—young and old, male and female, highborn and commoner—all were smiling, relaxed, with none of the stiff formality she associated with their time period.

There must have been nearly two hundred people aboard the Train's five cars...and plenty of room for more. Many, apparently, had boarded since the journey began. One elderly man introduced her to his grandparents, who were easily half his age; another family boasted four consecutive generations aboard the Train. In the smoking car Susan saw a poker game in progress between two great-grandfathers and their great-grandsons...all of whom were apparently the same age.

Professor Möbius' Time Distortion Engine, which occupied most of a luggage car directly behind the tender, was indeed a marvelous and complicated device. It was all composed of shining brass and copper tubing, massive spinning magnets, miles of tightly-wound wire, and blown glass structures twisted into odd shapes that did not seem to belong in the world at all. A deep purple glow played over the entire machine, and every few seconds electrical sparks danced along its surface. Being near the Time Distortion Engine gave Susan an odd feeling of discomfort in her stomach, as if she were on a roller coaster.

She wished Bob could be here to see it.

The Slow Train, Susan learned, was not bereft of modern technology—nor of knowledge of the outside world. They'd had radio, George told her, since the 1920s: some tinkerers had built a device that slowed down selected transmissions to match the Train's slow time. Newcomers and those re-boarding after an absence always brought along the latest books, magazines, and newspapers. A battered black-and-white television set, its chassis and tubes wired into the Train's electrical system, sputtered to itself at the rear of the smoking car; she imagined men huddled around it, catching quick glimpses of images from a world beyond their dreams.

"Harry tells me he's brought aboard a DVD player and a selection of movies," George told her. "I expect there will be great debate over what to watch first: *Casablanca* or *Star Wars*."

They told her that they were heading for Cornwall: the end of the line was Land's End, and if the Andrew kept them on schedule as he had so far, they expected to arrive near the end of the twenty-third century.

"And what will you do then?" she asked.

Maggie answered with a laugh. "Why, turn around and come back! What else?"

In the end, the allotted hour went far too quickly, and Susan found herself on the Train's rear platform unable to let go of George's hand. The luggage was all loaded, the tender had been replenished with wood from the tumble-down station, and the conductor was making a final walk back from the engine to the Train's tail.

"Gr—George," she said, "It's been wonderful. I'm sorry I doubted you. I don't know how to thank you for letting me see this."

His eyes met hers. "Susan...you're welcome to come along."

Her throat closed, and a sudden lump appeared in her chest. "I couldn't." Could she?

"It's your decision, my dear. I gather that you aren't as happy with Bob as you could be?"

"No, that's true." She looked out over the forgotten town of Coombe-on-Axe, tried to imagine going back to Bob, back to Baltimore, back to her job and her tiny apartment. Back to the arguments, the stress, the endless frustrations of modern life.

Why, when she could stay here and pass that life completely by?

George squeezed her hand. "It's your choice," he repeated. "I took the Slow Train to escape...and sometimes I wonder if I did the right thing." He smiled. "Then again, if I hadn't I would never have known the joys of my family, and of seeing my little girl grow up."

The conductor reached the end of the station's listing platform. His shout echoed in the still afternoon: "All aboard!"

I want to stay, Susan thought helplessly. It would be so easy; she didn't even have to move. The difficult choice was to stay; to jump off the Train and let it go chugging away into the future. Three metal steps stood between her and the real world, but those three steps might just as well have been a yawning chasm.

Bob wouldn't miss her, at least not for long.

The conductor swung a flag and sang out again, "All abooooard!"

As if struck by an electric shock, Susan moved suddenly, bent to kiss George on the cheek, and took a single step down. "Thank you, George, but I can't. I...I can't run away, not now. Not yet." Not until I've tried everything, not until I'm sure it won't work.

George nodded. "Good girl."

The Train lurched, and the conductor jumped aboard, tipping his hat to Susan. "All aboard, Miss," he said sweetly.

Susan moved down a step, then another. One more step would take her off the Train.

George reached into his suit jacket and thrust a large envelope at her. "Take these papers. I've put everything—the business, the houses, the cars—all in your name."

The Train started moving; a faltering, lurching movement as if the Train itself were reluctant to leave. Susan squeezed George's hand for the last time. "Thank you. I don't know what to say."

He let go. "How about 'See you soon?' Our next stop is Dunkeswell. I put the schedule in that packet."

She jumped off the last step, feeling a tingle as she landed on the stony ground. She heard the conductor call out destinations, in the fashion of conductors throughout history, "Dunkeswell, Butterleigh, Morchard Bishop, Taw Green..."

The Train pulled ahead, gathering speed as it moved away...two feet, then three, four, five....

"Susan!" George shouted. His voice was frantic. "Here, I almost forgot. Take this." Hanging on to the railing, he held another envelope out to her.

"...Highampton, St. Giles on the Heath, Upton Cross..."

She ran to the Train, grabbed at the envelope, and felt gravel shift. Her feet went out from underneath her. She fell to her knees and watched as the Train surged ahead as if finally catching its breath.

Then, suddenly, there was a ripple in the air, and the Train seemed to freeze, to grow slightly transparent even as it was moving away. There stood George, now a statue with his arm extended in farewell. There stood the conductor, his words still echoing the Train's path well into the next century: "... Cardinham, Hensbarrow Downs, Carland Cross, Three Burrows..."

In the sudden silence she was alone, except for a ghostly image on the tracks and a single envelope fluttering to a soft landing in the tall grass.

Just for the joy of the laughing, she laughed.

Standing gingerly on skinned knees, she picked up the envelope. It was creased and worn, and her name was scrawled across it in faded fountain pen. Whatever it was, George had been carrying it for years.

She tore it open and laughed all the harder when she saw the two stubby pieces of cardboard inside. They were, she knew, purely symbolic—but they were a gift more precious than all his bank accounts and houses and cars put together.

A pair of tickets, destination unspecified, for a ride on the one and only Slow Train.

Tucking the tickets in her pocket with the rest of the papers, she turned with a smile to the unhurried walk back to the car. Behind her, she heard the phantom voice of a train whistle echo from the hills.

AUTHOR'S NOTE

This tale was inspired by a song.

In the 1960s the British comedy duo Flanders and Swann wrote and performed "The Slow Train," a clever ode to discontinued British railway stations (the song is included on their 1964 album *At the Drop of Another Hat*). Some time later, the King's Singers released a haunting, wistful version of the same song. It certainly haunted me…after weeks of having the tune run through my head, I finally devised a science-fictional meaning to the phrase "the slow train."

I spent a few more weeks working out the background and route of the train, and then the story came fairly easily.

When *Analog's* editor, Stan Schmidt, bought the story, he told me that he was stretching the definition of "science fiction" about as far as he felt his readers would allow him…but he liked the story so much, he didn't care.

People have asked me if there will be more tales of the Slow Train, perhaps even a novel. I admit that the idea never occurred to me. But now that I'm prompted, I realize that the train is full of passengers…and all of them have their own stories. So I expect we haven't seen the last of the Slow Train.

The Scattered Worlds Mosaic by Don Sakers

Dance for the Ivory Madonna
a romance of psiberspace
Print & Kindle
Spectrum Award finalist; 56 Hugo nominations
"Imagine a Stand on Zanzibar written by a left-wing Robert Heinlein, and infused with the most exciting possibilities of the new cyber-technology." -Melissa Scott, author of Dreaming Metal, The Jazz

Weaving the Web of Days
a tale of the Scattered Worlds
Print & Kindle
Maj Thovold has led the Galaxy for three decades, a Golden Age of peace and prosperity. She is weary and ready to resign, but she faces one last battle: a battle on the strangest battlefield known: a web of living tendrils that stretches across interstellar space. A web where Maj's enemies wait, like spiders, for their prey....

The Eighth Succession
a novel of the Scattered Worlds
Print & Kindle
"Remember when science fiction used to be filled with galactic intrigue and bigger-than-life heroes? The wonderful Don Sakers certainly does! The Eighth Succession is a rip-roaring yarn, impossible to put down. If John W. Campbell's Astounding Stories had been published in an LGBT-friendly era, this is the cover-story serial you'd have been waiting anxiously for each month. What a ride!" -Robert J. Sawyer, Hugo Award-winning author of Red Planet Blues

Children of the Eighth Day
a novel of the Scattered Worlds
Print & Kindle
The Eighth Succession *introduced readers to the Hoister Family...*
Children of the Eighth Day *takes the story of this remarkable family to the exciting next level.*

The Scattered Worlds Mosaic by Don Sakers

All Roads Lead to Terra
two tales of the Scattered Worlds
Kindle only
Two exciting tales tell of attacks against the shining jewel of the Terran Empire: Earth. Includes an introduction and notes from the author.

A Voice in Every Wind
two tales of the Scattered Worlds
Print & Kindle
On a world where meaning lives in every rock and stream, and every breeze brings a new voice, one human explorer stands on the threshold of discoveries that could alter the future of Humanity.

A Rose From Old Terra
a novel of the Scattered Worlds
Print & Kindle
Jedrek left the Grand Library and his work circle eleven years ago. Now a crisis in uncharted space brings the circle back together. Soon, Jedrek and his friends are at the focal point of a clash of cultures, and the only thing that can save the Galaxy is one modest group of Librarians.

The Leaves of October
a novel of the Scattered Worlds
Print & Kindle
Compton Crook Award finalist
The Hlutr: Immensely old, terribly wise…and utterly alien. When mankind went out into the stars, he found the Hlutr waiting for him. Waiting to observe, to converse, to help. Waiting to judge…and, if necessary, to destroy.

More Books from Speed-of-C Productions

The Curse of the Zwilling by Don Sakers
Print & Kindle

It's Hogwarts meets Buffy at Patapsco University: a small, cozy liberal arts college like so many others – except for the Department of Comparative Religion, where age-old spells are taught and magic is practiced. When a favorite teacher is found dead under mysterious circumstances, grad student David Galvin finds that a malevolent evil has awakened. And now David, along with four novice undergrads, must defeat this ancient, malignant terror.

The SF Book of Days by Don Sakers
Print only

Drawn from the pages of classic sf literature, here is a science fiction/fantasy event for every day of the year...and for quite a few days that aren't *part of the year. From Doc Brown's arrival in Hill Valley (January 1, 1885) to the launch of the* Bellerophon *(Sextor 7, 2351), this datebook is truly out of this world.*

PsiScouts #1: At Risk by Phil Meade
Print & Kindle

In the 26th century, psi-powered teenagers from all over the Myriad Worlds join together as the heroic PsiScouts.

Meat and Machine: queer writings by Don Sakers
Print & Kindle

Don Sakers has been queering sf and fantasy for three decades. Meat and Machine collects 24 short pieces of Don's science fiction, fantasy, nonfiction, and erotics.

Five Planes by Melissa Scott & Don Sakers
Print & Kindle

Space opera adventure. Pirates. Judges. Weird physics. Desperate refugees. Struggling colonists. Missing persons and a mystery ship. A quest for human origins in a pocket universe.

More Books from Speed-of-C Productions

Gaylaxicon Sampler 2006
Print only
Sample the work of thirteen writers from across the spectrum of gay, lesbian, bisexual, and/or transgender science fiction, fantasy, and/or horror. Includes big names and small, much-published veterans and promising beginners, Lammy and Spectrum Award nominees and winners, past Gaylaxicon Guests of Honor, and fresh new names.

QSpec Sampler 2007
Print only
Originally prepared as a giveaway at Gaylaxicon 2007 in Atlanta, this volume is available at a nominal charge as a sampler of the fine work being done by GLBT writers in SF, fantasy, and horror.

Act Well Your Part by Don Sakers
Print & Kindle
A beloved gay young adult romance, back in print for its adult fans as well as a new generation of teens. At first Keith Graff dislikes his new school. He misses his old friends, and despairs of ever fitting in. Then he joins the school's drama club, and meets the boyishly cute Bran Davenport….

Lucky in Love by Don Sakers
Print & Kindle
A companion novel to Act Well Your Part, Lucky in Love *follows Keith's friend Frank, torn between bad boy Dwight and basketball star Darnell.*

A Cosmos of Many Mansions: Varieties of SF by Don Sakers
Print & Kindle
Based on the first five years of Sakers's popular review column, this volume examines & explains dozens of types of science fiction along with hundreds of reviews.

The Mud of the Place by Susanna J. Sturgis
Print only
*"A sensitive, witty, and tightly plotted portrayal of life on Martha's Vineyard that only a true Islander could have written.
Nice going, Susanna!" –Cynthia Riggs*

www.ingramcontent.com/pod-product-compliance
Lightning Source LLC
Chambersburg PA
CBHW061254170626
46809CB00007B/2997